Larry Thompson

SAID THE CREATURE FROM EPSILON ERIDANI TO NAPOLEON'S CAPTAIN:

"For centuries my people have lived in peace and have therefore completely forgotten the arts of war. Without proper programming, our computers are of no use to us. On several occasions airfleets directed by them have been utterly destroyed by the Kveyars.

"Since these demons from beyond our space frontiers give us no respite, we have to take fast action. Our computers have therefore advised that we search among the inhabited planets for a people who seem trained in the art of combat. Test observations show that your kind have a great deal of experience in this domain. And that is why we have come to look for a few individuals on Earth—in order to make them our military leaders."

SAID NAPOLEON'S CAPTAIN TO THE SPACE MONSTER:

"Fine! But before I agree, there are a number of points to be cleared up. To begin with. . . ."

GILBERT 76

Chapter One

A glacial wind whirled the snowflakes that slowly drifted down from a leaden sky. As far as the eye could see, the Russian steppes were being covered with a spotless mantle.

Winter had just begun and would be in full force for the next five months. It had started on November 6, 1812, when the retreating Imperial Army was between Vyazma and Smolensk.

The temperature immediately dropped and hovered around zero.

Never had Napoleon's troops been put to such a test. Leaving Moscow in triumph, their packs and pockets crammed with the fruits of pillage, they had started the long trek home with the conviction that they would quickly reach a still-undamaged city in which they could set up comfortable winter quarters.

There was soon an endless file of wagons and carriages snaking along the road. They had scarcely gone three leagues when a terrifying explosion made every head turn: the Kremlin had just blown up.

After only one day, many of the sumptuous vehicles in which the pillagers had thought they would be able to travel comfortably were already in trouble: the condition of the roads, churned up by the artillery caissons, had been too much for the axles.

The time had come to be more selective about the treasures being carried off. A few experienced, crusty veterans of the Old Guard took the opportunity to trade items of silverware and gold plate for furs and fur-lined cloaks, which once placed under their saddles would protect their horses from the already biting cold.

Those who did so easily reached the Moskva battlefield, on which innumerable corpses still lay unburied; then they managed to make it to Vyazma.

Surrounded by his Old Guard, the emperor advanced in slow stages. On the flanks of the interminable column, bands of shouting cossacks were ever on the watch; pitilessly eliminating stragglers and scouts. But the soldiers maintained their ranks and kept their weapons loaded, and those cossacks who were too daring soon found themselves stretched facedown before some old veteran nodding his head and tossing his rifle back on his shoulder.

The snow storm of November 6th and the cold wave quickly changed this orderly retreat into a rout. The horses began to die of exposure and hunger. The men, badly protected against the rigors of a Russian winter, soon followed.

In the grayish fog the weakened army units lost their cohesion and broke up. All the men could think about was fleeing this pitiless land as quickly as possible. Those who had had the foresight to load up with supplies rather than gold withstood these first tests relatively well. The luckiest were the hussars and cuirassiers whose mounts had managed to survive the storm. Leaving the foot soldiers behind, they were among the first to enter the hamlets and villages, where it was sometimes still possible to unearth food supplies forgotten in the isbas, the log huts. Most often they would find the place deserted: the Russian men, fearing the vengefulness of the retreating troops, had fled into the forests. Only a few women occasionally remained behind.

The most difficult problem for the retreating soldiers was not to get lost in the immensity of the featureless steppes. The snow-covered roads could no longer be distinguished from the fields, and the men had to estimate their direction from the sun whenever a pale ray managed to pierce the gray clouds.

Thus it was that a small troop of eight men mounted on sturdy horses slowly made their way toward Smolensk.

Their mounts sank into the soft snow up to their knees, slipping with every step despite the fact that

6

their iron shoes had long since been removed to give them a better purchase on the ground. Emerging from a pine wood, they were advancing toward a frozen lake; the slippery surface would make for easier going, since there were no hollows into which the poor beasts could sink.

All these three-chevroned soldiers wore warm, fur-lined capes on top of their overcoats, and the snow encrusted on their crested helmets, shakos, and busbys made them look like Christmas snowmen.

With hollow eyes sunken in their sockets, stalactites of ice hanging from their moustaches, they moved forward in complete silence. Only their vaporized breath proved that they were not phantoms.

At the head of this motley group was their leader, Captain Bernard. A tough-looking rascal whose gray eyes were constantly on the alert, he gripped his right hand firmly over the butt of his pistol, which he kept warm in the pocket of his superb zibeline pelisse. Born in Paris, he had been a dragoon in every campaign since the Directory. He was a remarkable horseman whose saber and lance had taken their toll as he charged at the head of his light cavalry, and so it was not surprising that he was one of the first to receive the Legion of Honor.

Behind him was his orderly, Friancourt. A fellow from the rough Menilmontant district in Paris, he was as outspoken and resourceful a man as you could find; nobody could beat him when it came to sniffing out a side of bacon or some smoked meats whenever they made a halt. He seemed to have the nose of a bloodhound. A redhead, his sumptuous, fiery beard had won him the nickname of Poil de Carotte, or Carrot Bristle.

Alongside him was Queunot, a chestnut-haired Breton of a pronounced Celtic type, who also belonged with the 28th Cavalry. Thin and wiry, he had unbelievable powers of resistance and never complained. These three were the only ones who belonged to the same outfit. The other members of their original company had melted into the vast grayness.

Behind them came two gunners: Bourief, a Belgian

from Brussels; and Chastel, an Alsatian from Colmar. Their four-gun battery had been lying sunk in a ditch near the Moskva for some time now. The red pompons on their shakos drooped sadly under the weight of the snow.

Kaninski, a Polish hussar, followed them. He spoke French, and he also spoke Russian very well, which was extremely valuable when they wanted to interrogate peasants who had been flushed from a cottage. The frost-encrusted black plume of his shako pointed boldly toward the sky.

Faultrier and Géraudont brought up the rear. Provisional horsemen, they belonged to the front-line infantry, the first as a surgeon, the second as a medic. The latter kept unhappily shifting around on his saddle because his bruised and aching posterior gave him no respite. . . .

When the frozen lake had cautiously been traversed, Captain Bernard made a slight detour to the right so that he could climb a small hill overlooking the neighboring plain. It was late afternoon and night was beginning to fall.

They all stopped here and, awkwardly wiping their eyes with their thick-gloved fingers, looked around for some recognizable landmark.

"Nothing!" grumbled Friancourt. "Not the slightest sign of life. *Saprelotte,* I would have given twenty francs to be able to sleep with a roof over my head!"

"We're going to have to camp here," muttered the officer. "These pine trees will give us something to make a fire with. We can improvise a hut with the boughs."

"Our horses are sure to be dead tomorrow if this cold keeps up," noted Faultrier, who had joined them. "The poor beasts haven't eaten in three days. If only we had stumbled upon a village!"

"Bah! As long as a man gets a little something to eat, he can manage somehow," Bourief said optimistically. "If the nags die, we'll cut a few steaks out of them. Nobody here would turn up his nose at that!"

"That's nonsense!" grumbled Chastel. "You'll see

when we have to advance on foot and your toenails freeze. If the animals die, we have had it!"

"And what about the cossacks?" added Géraudont. "If we have to proceed on foot, we'll never get away from them."

"Hold it!" interrupted Friancourt. "I think I see a thin column of smoke over there. . . ."

"Crazy Poil de Carotte! You're beginning to see things. . . ."

"No, really! Look over toward the west."

"I don't see a thing. . . ."

But at that very moment, a slight break in the clouds let through a golden shaft of the setting sun, and for a split second it caught a grayish mass that lay stagnant over a small valley. Scarcely had it been seen before it was dissipated by the wind, but the observers had had time to become convinced that a small village was nestled over there, a few versts away.

"Captain!" shouted Friancourt. "There's a hamlet or something up ahead. Maybe we can find shelter for the night."

"Maybe," mumbled the officer, laboriously detaching an icicle that hung from his moustache. "But how can we be sure that a squad of cossacks hasn't beat us to it? It might be like walking into a wolf's mouth."

"We could wait in the woods over there until twilight and then look it over carefully while our horses remain hidden in the shrubbery, couldn't we?"

"Damn! The poor nags sure could use a little food. With all this snow they haven't been able to smell out a thing to eat. Good old Volant here is ready to munch the thatch off a cottage roof! Let's hope we can find some hay over there."

"I promise to come up with everything they need, and maybe even a ham or two for us," Friancourt assured them. "Take my word for it—these damn muzhiks have piles of hidden supplies, and I'll get my hands on them somehow!"

"All right, that's a promise. I'm counting on you. Let's head toward the village. But keep on your toes."

The horsemen continued their slow advance under

the cover of the trees, whose lower branches inhibited their progress and showered them with snow whenever they brushed against them.

The men were riding along the edge of the wood, climbing a crest that dominated the little valley, when several black dots appeared and seemed to be coming right toward them. Bourief's sharp eyes made out about ten horsemen who looked as if they were fleeing the village behind them just as fast as they could.

"*Sacrénom!* Cossacks!" growled Bernard. "Dismount quickly! Get those horses down on the ground and check your pistols. Maybe they'll go by without spotting us. . . ."

These orders were carried out immediately.

It had begun to snow again, and the horses behind the bushes were soon invisible. The soldiers leaned back against the horses' trunks, and raising their rifles, drew a bead on the phantom forms that were rapidly looming larger. From time to time the men blew on their swollen fingers in an effort to warm them.

The captain's prediction turned out to be accurate. A troop of cossacks were coming from the village, and they were heading straight for the woods where the men were hidden.

"Let's avoid a fight if we can! No one is to fire unless I give the order," the officer said sharply. "The swine have been taking it easy in those isbas, and they're in fine shape. I can't say as much for us."

The men nodded to show they had understood; they poured priming powder into the vents of their pistols and rifles, then unsheathed their sabers and planted them in the snow before them. By now the cossacks were only some thirty yards away. As calmly as though they were on a parade ground, the soldiers placed their eyes against the sights of their weapons, vaguely regretting the long lances which had been abandoned so as not to overburden the horses.

The Russians seemed nervous and frequently turned in their saddles, as if to assure themselves that nobody was following them. They kept digging their spurs into their horses, and the poor beasts, nostrils fuming and

10

froth dripping from their mouths, made desperate efforts to trot through the soft snow. The first six horsemen passed without spotting the Frenchmen hidden behind the trees. The seventh, however, saw Bourief and pointed a lance at him, uttering a guttural cry. Bernard stiffened, ready to give the order to fire, but to his amazement the leader of the cossacks paid no attention to the men who had been pointed out to him. Instead, he continued on his way and signaled the other horsemen to follow.

The French captain could not get over his astonishment. Never had cossacks refused a similar invitation to combat! They would often back off when an adversary appeared tough and determined to sell his life dearly, but they would always charge at least once before giving up their quarry. Therefore, fearing some trick, Bernard ordered his little band to stay in position.

They all kept their eyes on the cossacks, expecting at every moment to see them wheel about, but the horsemen and their mounts continued to show their backs to the soldiers and were soon gone, swallowed up by the gray twilight.

"At ease!" ordered Bernard. "Sling arms!"

Then he added pensively, "I wonder why they didn't even pay us the courtesy of a single shot."

"Maybe they've just been given a going-over by some of our boys," suggested his orderly, taking a well-seasoned pipe from his pocket.

"That would only have been possible if this village had been occupied by a detachment of chasseurs or light cavalry," put in Faultrier, who had just come up to them. "We haven't wasted our time since Vyazma and the line infantry is way behind us."

"It's possible," agreed the captain. "Strange that we haven't come across any trace of them—but after all, with this damn snow every trail is quickly covered over."

"How about a snort, Captain?" asked Géraudont, pulling a flask out of his pocket.

"Thanks. I'm not the man to say no. That's the best of all those medicines you cart around!"

11

"It could be," interjected Bourief, "that for once in their lives our boys took the direct route, couldn't it? We've had to circle around quite a bit because of this storm."

"Yes," agreed Chastel, "that's very possible. But I don't like this at all. Cossacks have more than one trick up their sleeves. I'll bet a barrel of sauerkraut the bastards are setting a trap for us!"

Bernard thought for a moment while he vigorously scratched his neck. In spite of the cold a few lice must have survived in the comparative warmth of his crested helmet. He stared morosely at the flakes that were falling more and more thickly, and then said:

"One thing is sure. We can't spend the night out-doors, or by morning our horses will be buried under five feet of snow. We'd better keep moving. Queunot, you get out front as a scout, but be sure to keep us in sight at all times. We're going to investigate that village."

"At your orders, Captain," snapped the Breton as he led his horse out of the bushes. The horse snorted and shook off the layer of spotless snow that had covered him. Queunot grabbed the cantle of his saddle, hoisted himself into the seat, and, digging in his heels, disappeared into the icy mist.

The other soldiers followed his example, and the little troop rode out of the cover provided by the trees. They all frequently looked uneasily over their shoulders, astonished not to see the cossacks come riding back. But the Russians evidently had no interest in them and did not reappear. For the next ten minutes or so the horsemen followed along behind their scout, eventually arriving at a hollow at the bottom of which was a small settlement—at most twenty isbas—sunk in the fog.

Queunot was waiting for them. Pointing to a path which wound down the side of the valley, he said:

"I haven't spotted a thing, Captain. There's some smoke coming out of a few chimneys, but I don't think any of our people are down there. Not that I can see much now that it's getting dark."

"All right. Stay some distance ahead of us," said Bernard. He took a spyglass out of his saddlebags, slowly scrutinized the hamlet, then closed the instrument with a sharp click and carefully stored it away again.

"Nothing special?" asked Faultrier.

"No! Even supposing that one of our detachments has taken up quarters in this village, it can't be a very large one. There's no sign of anything outside the cottages."

"In one way that's all to the good," Géraudont said jokingly. "I hate getting to an inn and being told that there's no room!"

The horsemen spurred their mounts and began a cautious descent. The path sloped gently around the hill and the horses didn't slide too badly.

"Christ!" grumbled Kaninski, blowing on his fingers in an effort to warm them up. "Winter in the Carpathians is none too warm, but *kurva,* it can't begin to compare with this!"

"Don't let it get you down," Bourief said reassuringly. "For a change, within ten minutes we'll be in a nice warm isba."

"I can almost smell that bacon frying now," Géraudont said dreamily. "Throw in a few nicely browned potatoes and I'll be satisfied."

"Not me," said Chastel, touching up the dream. "I want a nice warm haystack to curl up in and go to sleep."

"Shut up, can't you!" Faultrier said in irritation. "Talk of something else for a change. You'll bring us bad luck."

"Say, Major," noted Friancourt, "I think my ears are frostbitten. . . ."

"Rub them with a handful of snow, imbecile!"

The chasseur reined in for a moment next to a bush, and pushing his hair away from his ears, rubbed them vigorously with snow.

They rode along in silence for a while, and then at a turn in the path the captain saw Queunot signaling them to join him. They all reined in alongside the scout.

13

"If I may say so, Captain, I think I heard something up ahead. It sounded like high-pitched voices, but they couldn't have been French voices, in any case. It almost sounds as though somebody's climbing up the path."

"Quiet!" ordered Bernard, cupping a hand to his ear.

For a moment, none of them heard a thing. The thick layer of snow covering the countryside deadened all noise as effectively as cotton wadding.

Then the sounds reached them, and they could hear squabbling voices very clearly.

"Could be Russian," noted the captain. "Do you catch anything, Kaninski?"

The latter signaled for silence and then, after listening intently for a few moments, replied:

"*Da*, Captain! Women! They must be from the village, and the little doves have had a bad scare. They're saying something about a big pot that has fallen from the sky. . . ."

"You're drunk! What nonsense," grumbled Bernard. "A flying pot? Talk sense, will you?"

"Sorry, sir. Perhaps I did misunderstand, but we'll know soon enough, because they're coming this way."

A few minutes later a small group of women came around a turn in the path and stood before the horsemen, who as a precaution had raised their rifles to their shoulders. Strangely enough, the peasant women showed no terror at the sight of the Frenchmen. On the contrary, they seemed much relieved by this unexpected meeting. The wretched creatures had enormous shawls over their heads and shoulders, but they weren't at all dressed for a nocturnal expedition in such freezing weather. Several of them were even walking through the snow barefooted, as though in their haste to escape some unknown peril they hadn't even taken the time to put on their fur-lined boots.

There were eight in all, relatively young, and some even pretty, at least as far as could be made out in the deepening twilight.

"Ask them why they've come," Bernard ordered Kaninski.

He put a few questions to the woman who seemed

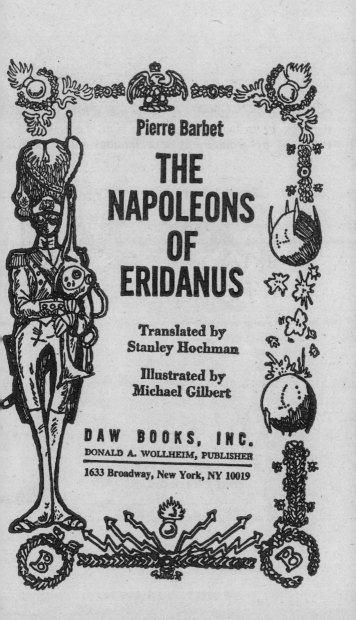

Pierre Barbet

THE NAPOLEONS OF ERIDANUS

Translated by
Stanley Hochman

Illustrated by
Michael Gilbert

DAW BOOKS, INC.
DONALD A. WOLLHEIM, PUBLISHER

1633 Broadway, New York, NY 10019

FIRST PRINTING, JUNE 1976

3 4 5 6 7 8 9

 DAW TRADEMARK REGISTERED
REGISTRADA. HECHO EN U.S.A.
U.S. PAT. OFF. MARCA

PRINTED IN U.S.A.

the oldest member of the group and she replied briefly, pointing her finger at a spot close to the village, which was now masked by the trees. Her companions joined in a chorus, trying to outdo one another in squealing corroboration of what she had said.

The Pole seemed perplexed; he rubbed his nose and then said somewhat uncertainly: "Captain, I don't want you to think that I'm trying to be funny or anything, but it's just what I was saying a little while ago. A big pot landed near the isbas, falling out of the sky with a screech that sounded as if all the devils in hell had started up together. And then there was something like a flaming sword in the clouds. Once the thing had landed, the snow around it melted. The cossacks had been there and ordered the muzhiks to take their pitchforks and follow them. Pikes and manure forks at the ready, they went up to this devil's pot. The women remained in the rear, watching. At first, nothing happened, but when the poor bastards got within ten feet of the thing, the iron tools they were carrying began to crackle, and blue flames started shooting from them. It looked to the women as though the men couldn't drop the cursed things, and whatever it was that was happening evidently burned like hell. The men's hair and beards were stiff, and blue sparks kept shooting out of them. Except for a few cossacks, all the men took to their heels. They just ran off without waiting to find out any more. The women brought out their icons, but there seemed to be no way to get the better of this devil. In fact, beams of light suddenly began searching for the women, who kicked up their heels and ran to hide themselves in the woods just as fast as their legs would carry them."

"That sounds absurd, doesn't it? They're probably trying to pull our legs. After all, we would have been able to hear that damn pot come screeching down. Tell them what I said, and see what they have to say."

Kaninski asked a few more questions, to which the Russian women replied without any apparent hesitation.

"Well, it's this way, Captain. According to them, the thing fell more than two hours ago. At first they all—

the women as well as the cossacks—just looked at it and wondered what would come out. They saw forklike things spinning around on top of it, and then lights went on. After about an hour or so, a kind of door opened. The cossacks began to argue among themselves, and after a few belts of vodka to put some heart into them, they finally made up their minds to go closer. That's when the lightning began playing around the tips of their lances and the pitchforks of the peasants. . . ."

"Bah! What a story," said Bernard, pulling on a lock of hair over his left temple. "What do you make of it, Faultrier?"

"Ma foi," replied the surgeon. "If you ask me, the story seems to hold together. The cossacks aren't raw recruits, and the ones we saw seemed to have had a bad scare. The best thing would be for us to go and take a look. After all, we don't have much to lose."

"Just what I think! Let's get moving. Kaninski, tell these women to follow us. Dressed the way they are, they'd never survive a night outdoors."

The Pole transmitted the invitation, but the ladies didn't seem any too eager to obey. Before they could be brought to agree, they had to be threatened with the sabers. Even then they insisted on only serving as guides, reclaiming their freedom as soon as the devil's pot came into sight.

Shrugging his shoulders, Bernard agreed, and the little troop began moving forward in the dark.

Chapter Two

Only the slight twilight glow from the west enabled the horsemen to make out the path which gently sloped toward the valley.

On each side of them a wall of snow-covered pines looked like a gigantic guard of honor. The troopers, made uneasy in spite of themselves by the women's stories, kept their eyes wide open to see if the much-talked-about pot was real or simply the fruit of these peasant women's imaginations. Judging from the way the women behaved, something very strange must have happened; they were huddled together like terrified beasts.

Finally, after the last turn in the path had been made, the soldiers could see for themselves. Before them, lighting up the snow with a soft bluish glow, was the devilish pot or kettle. The thing really did have a shape that recalled this commonplace utensil set upside down on the ground, with four rods that looked like legs.

Bernard signaled his companions to stop, and soothingly stroked the neck of his stallion, which had also seen the contraption and was showing signs of nervousness.

"Strange," he murmured, turning to Faultrier. "The women were telling the truth. . . . What could it be? It looks as though it's on fire, but the snow isn't melting!"

The surgeon seemed extremely perplexed, and scratching his chin he replied hesitantly: "Maybe it's some kind of hot-air balloon. I seem to remember that balloons were used in several military campaigns: in General Pichegru's siege of Mayence in '94, and in the siege of Mantua in '95. I believe even the French army in Egypt had some balloons, but they were lost in Aboukir. . . ."

"Of course, damn it! What a fool I am!" exploded the captain. "Obviously it's some kind of balloon! We found one in Moscow. A German named Leppich had built it so that they could bombard our army. The Little Corporal had it burned, but the Russians probably have others. Now I understand why these poor savages were so terrified when they saw it fall from the sky."

"But whatever could have happened to its passengers? I don't see the gondola," the doctor continued.

The officer took out his spyglass and inspected the presumed balloon at great length. Meanwhile, the Russian women, somewhat reassured at seeing these damned *Franzuskiies* laugh, tried to outshout one another as they asked Kaninski for explanations. Seduced by curiosity, they no longer even thought of slipping away.

"Quiet, you magpies!" growled Bernard as he carefully replaced the optical instrument in its case before speaking again. "No, there's no trace of a gondola. And there's something strange about the light. It looks as if the balloon is illuminated from inside. . . ."

"Oh! there's nothing very extraordinary about that. When the emperor's coronation was celebrated in 1804 they launched a free-flight balloon carrying an imperial crown made of phosphorescent glass. This is probably something similar that's used for night landings."

"Of course! I didn't know about that, but from what you tell me there's no question about it. Well, the thing for us to do now is to capture this contraption! And damn it," he concluded with a hearty laugh, "if it's still in working order, we can use it to get home by way of air! All right, there, let's move on, you bunch of loafers. . . ."

Very much at ease now due to the optimism of their leader, the troopers rode forward, curiously inspecting the balloon as they went. The women hadn't understood much, but they followed behind.

"Still and all, it's pretty big," noted the captain.

"From a distance I wouldn't have thought it so voluminous."

"I'm sure it's almost as high as the towers of Notre Dame," agreed the surgeon in an admiring tone. "I didn't think these muzhiks were capable of building anything like this!"

"Alas, my friend, neither did I ever think I would ever have to retreat through snow and glacial wind. This is one time our Little Corporal has overreached himself. In any case, the important thing is for us to be able to find shelter for the night. We'll puncture this bag of wind, then we'll take some well-earned rest in the isbas."

In spite of his seeming confidence, Bernard was still a bit suspicious of this very unusual mechanism that chance had placed in his path. Before deciding to go any closer, therefore, he made a large detour so that he could go around the thing.

Since they were now close to the isbas, the women went off to hide behind the clay-daubed walls in order to have relative protection should the pot act up again.

The soldiers, keeping a firm grip on their sabers, inspected the balloon for signs of anything unusual. The soft bluish light made it easy enough to see that the smooth surface of the device was unbroken except for the four "feet" pointing to the sky.

They had almost made a complete circuit of the balloon when Géraudont, who was up front with the captain, reined in his horse and let out of cry of surprise.

"Look, an opening. . . ."

"Yes, it's a kind of rectangular door. How can that be? The gas would escape through such an opening!"

"Unless the gondola is covered with cloth in order to protect the balloonists from the cold. . . ."

"That's always possible. In any case, the best way to find out is to go in. Stay here, I'm going to take a look through that door."

The captain dismounted, gave his reins to Géraudont, then, tightly gripping the butt of his pistol—which he had carefully checked to make sure it was

19

primed—approached noiselessly, alert for any un-pleasant surprise.

His heavy boots slid across the ground, and he observed that the snow had melted and turned to ice, which would seem to corroborate what the village women had told him. A few yards from his goal, Bernard paused a moment: he had just noticed that a kind of inclined plane, of extraordinary transparency, made it possible to reach the door, which was somewhat above ground level.

Since he saw nothing unusual, the captain moved forward again. A long corridor stretched before him. The officer bravely put his foot on the gangway, testing it before going any farther. It didn't sag under him at all, and he had no trouble in reaching the gaping aperture.

Once there, he stopped again. The corridor led into the bowels of the mysterious mechanism and seemed to go right to its center. On both sides closed doors could be distinguished, and a gentle warmth reigned in the interior of the balloon. The sensation was such an agreeable one after the rigors of the last few days that Bernard no longer hesitated, and he penetrated to the heart of the mechanism. There was no sign of anyone.

Obviously these damned Russians have managed to put together a really extraordinary apparatus, the captain thought. *No sign of a stove of any kind, and yet the temperature inside is positively summerlike!*

He mechanically ran his fingers along a nearby partition and noted with astonishment that it was made of neither cloth nor skin but of a substance that was hard, resistant, yet soft to the touch.

That explains why the balloon is so big, he thought. *It would have to be, since the gondola must weigh a ton.*

A few feet farther along the corridor he came to a door with a round knob and made a vain attempt to open it.

As the most absolute calm reigned, the officer returned to the door and signaled his men to join him. They all dismounted, and confiding their horses to Friancourt, they climbed aboard the strange machine.

"Christ!" whispered the surgeon when he had rejoined Bernard. "You'd think it was the middle of August! I haven't been this warm since we left France."

"You're right," agreed Bernard, "but I can't figure out how they heat it. Are you sure this is a balloon? The partitions seem very solid to me!"

"*Ma foi*, I'm not very sure of anything anymore," said Faultrier, pushing his shoulder against the wall. "This gondola must weigh a hell of a lot!"

"Exactly what I was thinking. . . ."

"Bah! Let's look around a little. I wish we could get this door open. Maybe we'd find something to eat inside."

"I've already tried, but I can't get that knob to turn."

"Did you? We'll soon see. . . ."

The doctor tried to turn the knob, then beat against the panel with his shoulder. Nothing happened.

"It must be bolted from inside. Let's see what we can find elsewhere."

The two officers, followed by the other men, went deeper into the apparatus. They tried every door they came to, but none would open. Since the temperature remained mild, one after the other began loosening his fur-lined coat to make himself more comfortable.

The corridor was enormous, and four men could walk abreast in it without getting in one another's way.

As the snow on their clothes melted, it formed little puddles on the smooth floor, but strangely enough the water seemed to be absorbed immediately, as though the floor covering were porous. Once the floor was dry, a strong breeze would sweep away the dust, and soon both floor and corridor were again immaculate. But the soldiers were too absorbed by other things to notice this phenomenon, for they had at last found a door that opened at the first try, and the spectacle inside was more than enough to catch and hold their attention. . . .

They gaped in wonder at a vast room whose walls were covered with vivid paintings. There were deep, soft chairs around tables laden with strange, brightly colored foods that seemed to beckon to them invitingly. The room was big enough to hold an entire company, but there was nobody inside. . . .

"Good Lord!" exclaimed Géraudont when the first moment of surprise had passed. "It looks like Sleeping Beauty's castle!"

"Doesn't it, though," said Bernard in a perplexed tone. "This can't possibly be a balloon: the gondola would be too heavy to lift. In any case, there's no need to look farther for a place in which to spend the night—we might as well settle in right here. But careful! On your toes! For the time being, nobody's to eat any of this! Queunot, tell Friancourt to send those village women here. Bring the horses into the corridor so that the poor beasts can warm up. After you've done that, remain on guard duty near the entrance. When the others have eaten, I'll see to it that you're relieved. Kaninski will go with you."

"At your orders, Captain," said Queunot, saluting. Then he made a regulation half-turn and went off to execute a mission that inspired little enthusiasm in him, since the gentle warmth of the room make him reluctant to confront the glacial night once more.

"Sacristi!" swore the surgeon, letting himself drop into one of the comfortable armchairs. "Life is full of surprises! This morning I wouldn't have given much for our chances of spending the night in a warm place. Look at those fruits, will you! They're really strange— especially for this time of year. *Saprelotte!* I've never seen anything like them. And those multicolored cubes look just like Turkish Delight."

"Don't touch them. Let the women have a few first and then we'll see," murmured Bernard. "I can't help being suspicious about this contraption and everything that's in it. Look around and make sure that nobody's hiding anywhere," he told his men. "If you find another door that opens, call me."

"Bah!" interjected the surgeon. "There's nobody here. The Russians have taken off, so it obviously doesn't belong to them, and it's a sure thing that our people didn't bring the thing here."

22

"That's exactly what worries me!"

"Maybe it was built at the whim of some prince or archduke."

"And what if the women were telling the truth? Suppose it really did come from the sky?"

"Hold on, now! This metal contrivance is much too heavy to fly. Take it easy, relax."

So saying, the surgeon set the example. Taking off his pelisse, he spread it over the back of a chair to dry. Next went his dark blue cape and bicorne, and then he began unbuttoning his dolman. As his boots came off, he uttered a sigh of relief.

Though he continued to glance about suspiciously, Bernard followed the doctor's example. As a precaution, however, he placed his two pistols in front of him on a low table and leaned his rifle against the arm of his chair. Only then did he decide to profit from the comfort of the place, and he finally unbuttoned his forest-green jacket and opened his collar with scarcely dissimulated pleasure. Then he removed his heavy crested helmet, the black plume of which was impregnated with water, and vigorously scratched his scalp. While he was doing all this the men came back from their inspection.

"Nothing to report, Captain," declared Bourief. "For once there's nobody."

"Did you follow the corridor to its end?"

"Yes, sir. It ends in a kind of shaft that goes to some upper level, but there are no stairs and the walls are too smooth to be able to climb."

"All right. Mount guard in the corridor."

During this exchange, Faultrier had gone up to the curious paintings that covered the walls of the room, and now he was looking at them in astonishment.

"What do you know about that! The relief on these things is so well done that I was almost fooled. Mother of God! The landscape seems so real that I can even smell the flowers! But they're unusual-looking. . . . I've never seen anything like them."

"You're right! That Russian prince of yours must

have very skillful artists in his employ, and that's another thing that worries me. . . ."

As he said this, they heard the sound of footsteps in the corridor and Kaninski came back with the others. They all had their arms loaded down with bottles and smoked hams. A few were even carrying sugarloaves and jars of muscovado.

"Well, now," laughed the captain, "it looks as though you haven't been wasting your time!"

"My Lord, those little doves were so surprised to see us take over this kettle without even firing a shot that we were able to persuade them to offer us a few tidbits. They think we must be sorcerers or something!"

"So much the better! Congratulations, boys! Come on in. Make yourselves comfortable and get some dinner ready for me. My stomach's sunk down to my heels!"

"We're going to cook up something really tasty, Captain," Friancourt assured him. "Just give us time to get a fire going outside. Queunot's working on it."

"Good. Give him a hand, but keep an eye out for trouble. We wouldn't want the cossacks to take us by surprise."

As the men settled down, they cheerfully hummed "The Straggler's March" and from time to time helped themselves to a little vodka. Soon they were all chorusing the Napoleonic anthem "Let Us Watch Over the Empire's Health."

Until now, the village women had timidly remained in the corridor, but attracted by the noise, they soon peeped through the doorway and then, gaining courage, entered the huge room.

Everything that's been said about the prestige of a uniform hasn't been just mere talk. As long as the troopers had their pelisses on, there was nothing very attractive about them. Now, however, the splendor of their outfits made a dazzling impression.

Chastel, for example, wore a navy-blue shoulder cape with a fur collar, shiny ornaments, scarlet trimmings, and red epaulettes that set off his dark complexion. Géraudont, as a carabineer, wore a white jacket and breeches that were still relatively clean, and his pompon-topped busby made him seem even taller than he was.

Kaninski, a Slav, had all that was needed to charm the sprightly villagers, and his sumptuous hussar's uniform attracted glances from the ladies. And in truth, these brilliant horsemen had always been the most colorfully outfitted soldiers of the Empire. Spruce and hearty, they were careful about their reputation and took pride in their elegance. The Pole, in spite of difficult conditions, knew how to appear at his best. His shoulder cape with its sky-blue ornaments, his rows of shining frogs and loops, his azure jacket, were spotless. In addition, he knew the art of sweeping his leg around so that his sabertache seemed to float in the air, and he also knew how to set off the shape of his legs with tight-fitting breeches decorated with gold braid.

The men were beginning to feel the effects of the heady wines brought back from the village, and they greeted the women with cries of encouragement.

"Come in, my pretties!" exclaimed Géraudont when he saw them. "Come and have a seat. You've really spoiled us, and it's only right that you should profit!"

"Here," added another soldier, grabbing up a platter of appetizing foods. "Try some of this, won't you, and let me know what you think of it!"

A bit intimidated, the women looked in amazement at the strange furnishings and the enormous paintings that seemed like windows opening onto a sunny landscape or forest. But since the Frenchmen behaved as though all this were the most natural thing in the world, they quickly relaxed and started to nibble away at some of the offered tidbits, evidently finding them quite tasty.

Bernard, who was watching them closely, murmured somewhat cynically so that only the doctor could hear him: "In any case, if a trap has been set by poisoning the food, the women are not in on it."

"My dear Captain," replied Faultrier, "you completely disgust me! As do all those whose profession it is to rip one another's guts out for reasons that may or may not be valid. If, like myself, you had to care for the poor bastards whose limbs have been hacked off and who are shrieking with pain, you might have a little more respect for human life!"

"Come, now," protested the officer, "there's no point in getting angry. You know that I'm not a butcher and that I'm as careful as I can be with the lives of my men. But what do you expect me to do? If this food is edible, we'll be able to take some with us—and damn it, there's no denying we need it! We've still got a hell of a long way to go before we get home."

"Oh, I'm not angry with you. I'm just a little tired of all this pointless slaughter. A lot we've accomplished up to now! Three-quarters of the Grand Army have been left behind, frozen on the Russian steppes, where in the spring they'll begin to rot. We'll never be able to fight off the coalition of allies. France has been bled white. We should never have launched such a venture!"

"Listen, old friend—I'm not interested in arguing on an empty stomach. Since our guests seem to have survived these goodies, I'm going to try a few myself."

Upon which, the officer grabbed a vermilion fruit with a rather wrinkled skin and bit off a mouthful.

"Mmm! Delicious! It tastes a little like a peach."

"I'll try some later," replied the surgeon. "I prefer to begin with a thick slice of ham. That at least is food for Christians!"

During this time the soldiers continued to extend themselves in doing the honors of the place to their guests. They unbuttoned their uniforms to make themselves more comfortable, and then they removed the kerchiefs from the heads of their guests so as to have a more accurate idea of their charms.

Kaninski, always the gallant and charming one, made it his business to concoct a mixture of vodka and some amber-colored liquid that was in flexible containers standing on the table. He began offering it around.

The beverage was greatly appreciated and its inventor complimented on his initiative. Bernard had also had a glass and now felt agreeably euphoric. Turning to the Pole, he exclaimed:

26

"Say, soldier, how about a little consideration for your comrades! Introduce us to these lovely ladies. You must know them pretty well by now, considering the amount of time you've been cooing with them. Damn it, I wish I knew what they were jabbering about!"

Kaninski didn't wait to be asked twice and immediately brought the Russian women to where the two officers were sitting. The group included blondes and two redheads—ordinary enough but lively and healthy-looking girls, of a type accustomed to work hard for a mere pittance, but whose white blouses and brightly colored skirts lent them a certain charm.

Two of them, Tania and Katia, were even real beauties, with their heavy tresses, fresh complexions, and sensual mouths.

Without further ado, Bernard grabbed Tania by the arm and made her sit alongside him on a pneumatically comfortable couch.

"Come, my little dove, come sit here! I have a feeling that we're going to get along very well, you and I."

And so saying he gave her an affectionate tap on the thigh and offered a reddish-brown fruit.

"Here, my beauty, bite into this and enjoy yourself. Kaninski," he called out, "what do I have to say so that she'll understand that I find her charming?"

"Call her *golubutchka,* Captain!"

"What's that again?"

"*Golubutchka*—little dove!"

"Well, then, *golubutchka* Tania, tonight you're my guest. Come on, Faultrier, choose one of the ladies and stop pretending to be shy. I know you, you old lecher!"

The surgeon gallantly rose, and bowing before the beautiful Katia signaled her to sit in the chair alongside his own.

"Watch it!" scolded the captain. "No touch pistols, right? If you do, I'll be angry. Kaninski, tell them what I said."

The Pole translated, but the two women laughingly protested and without a hint of bashfulness put their arms around the two officers' necks and kissed them full on the mouth to show that their intentions were friendly.

"That's more like it," chuckled Bernard. "Well, it was warm enough at Marengo, but I have a feeling that in a little while nobody will be freezing here. This one's not bad," he said, turning to Faultrier. "I wouldn't mind making her my regular bill of fare. . . ."

The surgeon seemed to be in complete agreement, but he had no time to give his opinion, since at that moment Queunot and Friancourt made their entrance carrying a big pot filled to the brim with a kind of cabbage and ham soup from which wafted a savory odor.

"That's not possible!" exclaimed Chastel in ecstasy. "It smells like sauerkraut! What a treat!"

"Good old Friancourt." The captain chuckled. "I knew you'd come through once again. Let's sit down at the table. I could eat a house."

Seeing the somewhat disappointed face of Queunot, who was returning to his guard post at the entrance to the corridor, he said to him:

"You look as uncomfortable as a Hungarian grenadier! You'll get your share soon. Take a snack along with you meanwhile—but keep a weather eye open!"

Chapter Three

Little by little the soldiers started making themselves as comfortable as possible. They unbuttoned their jackets and waistcoats, took off their boots, and adding the supplies found in the room to those discovered in the Russian village, began a gargantuan feast. They had eaten very little since their departure from Moscow, and now they were able to stuff themselves to the gills. They vaguely regretted not having a few mugs of warm wine, but they contented themselves with mixtures made of vodka.

Accustomed to heating their mess kits hastily over a wood fire and eating before their food was properly hot, they now licked their lips over the strange but exquisite taste of the victuals found in their unusual balloon.

Until he knew more, Bernard had decided to stick to the "balloon" explanation with his men. There would be time enough to set them straight later if it should prove necessary. In any event, since the place was comfortable and warm, and since no cossacks were around, what more could they want?

The hit of the evening was an enormous bucket of rum-spiked tea prepared by Lisa, one of the village women. Everyone present on that memorable occasion was given a dipperful of the incendiary brew, and the tempo of the proceedings increased considerably. Luckily, the dishes they had found in the room proved to be absolutely indestructible.

Bourief had replaced Queunot in the corridor, where the couples frequently strolled to stretch their legs a little. The horses stabled there had not been forgotten; a little forage had been supplied by the women, and the

29

worthy beasts were enjoying in complete tranquility a comfort they had long lost the habit of.

The captain and the surgeon had also partaken of the food and drinks, and having found a little tobacco at the bottom of their saddlebags, they were now ecstatically puffing away at their pipes, afloat in a beatific euphoria. Seated on their knees, Tania and Katia permitted themselves to be stroked like cats and purred with pleasure.

A few of the other men showed themselves more enterprising; hands insinuated themselves into blouses, and from time to time a startled beauty would laughingly flee the room, and a purely formal chase would take place in the long corridor.

And so it happened that one of the Russian women, Svetlana, made an important discovery: the doors, which until then had refused to open, finally ceded; all one had to do to make them work was to place a hand before an invisible light beam situated between the two vertical members of the frame.

Urged on by feminine curiosity, Svetlana took advantage of her discovery to explore beyond the door in the company of her admirer, and as they soon came to a rotunda covered with a spongy substance that was very pleasant to stretch out on, they weren't heard from for quite a while.

Their friends, who had observed how Svetlana had opened the door, profited from the discovery to wander off into all the rooms of this gondola, the dimensions of which were really astonishing.

Bernard and Faultrier were suddenly alone with the two Russian women, and they saw no reason to complain about the situation. . . .

However, if the captain's brain had been clearer, he might have avoided an adventure that was to cause him considerable perplexity.

It wasn't that the soldiers ran into any trouble. The only one who did was Géraudont, who almost broke his nose by racing head down into what had seemed to him a forest filled with shady nooks but which was actually an extremely realistic *trompe l'oeil* behind a screen of thick glass.

The one most responsible for the memorable events that befell the joyous revelers was Kaninski. Blessed with an extremely beautiful bass voice, he adored bel canto and played the piano rather well. Quite by accident his wanderings led him to a room whose walls were covered with what seemed to be innumerable clocks; in the center of the room was an unfamiliar keyboard instrument.

The hussar immediately tried to play some scales. . . .

But since no sound came from the instrument, Kaninski shrugged his shoulders and gave up. Renouncing the attempt to charm the gentle Ludmilla by a rush of harmony, he decided to demonstrate his tendernesss by more classic means.

None of the party noticed anything out of the ordinary at the time. The only thing was that Queunot, who was again on guard at the entryway to the corridor, almost had his foot crushed when a panel suddenly descended from the ceiling and hermetically sealed the opening. Somewhat surprised, the soldier leaned his rifle—a model from the Year IV—against the wall and ran his hands over the smooth panel. Perplexed at seeing himself so suddenly isolated from the outside world, he began to scratch the base of his neck. Not knowing what else to do, he grabbed up his rifle and growled: "Who goes there?"

Since nobody replied, he decided to give the alert by bawling out: "Cossacks!"

The rum-spiked tea distributed by his comrades had clouded his judgment, which was rather remarkable on ordinary occasions.

The familiar cry reverberated in the corridor and galvanized the energies of the men, who, without wasting any time in readjusting their uniforms, grabbed their weapons and came running to the rescue.

Bernard and Faultrier were the first to arrive on the scene, followed shortly thereafter by the others. The last to show up was Kaninski, who appeared bawling at the top of his voice:

"We'll run them through
Ran, ran, ran rantanplan, baff
Rantanplan baff in the face.
We'll run them through
And then we'll laugh!"

At first, the captain saw nothing unusual, and he began to haul Queunot over the coals for playing the clown.

For a few moments the sentry couldn't get a word in edgewise, but when the captain paused for breath he managed to explain. Then Bernard saw for himself that the corridor was in effect hermetically sealed, and he was none too happy about it.

"Sacrébleu!" he thundered. "We're caught like rats in a trap. You damn imbecile, didn't you see anybody?"

"Nobody, Captain, on my word of honor!"

"Well, that door didn't just close all by itself! Never mind, we'll discuss this later! Let's break this panel down!"

The soldiers backed off and hurled themselves against the panel, but it was no use. They bruised their shoulders without so much as budging it. Some other way would have to be found.

But bayonets used in an attempt to probe the seams broke without leaving so much as a scratch on the panel, which was made of some material as smooth as glass.

Increasingly desperate, the officer had three of the horses backed against the panel so that they could lash out against it with their hooves. This proved no more efficacious, as even their unshod hooves kept slipping off the panel as they flailed away more and more wildly. They were nevertheless kept at the hopeless task for quite a while.

Wondering what could be the cause of all the hubbub, the women clustered in the rear of the corridor. Kaninski eventually explained to them what the trouble was, and it was then that Svetlana told Bernard of how she had been able to open the other unyielding doors.

The captain slid his hand over the panel, but it seemed as insensible to caresses as to blows.

Redirecting his fury, the officer then began to call down his subordinates for not having told him about the door immediately, and turning on his heels, he led his little troop on a formal inspection of the rooms.

They noted that on either side of the central corridor there were eight triangular rooms and that none of them were any different from the one they had come across first. They seemed to be large recreation rooms with vividly colored paintings that created the impression of even greater spaciousness. Only the room containing the instrument which Kaninski had taken for a piano was somewhat different. Once more, Bernard was very perplexed.

"What do you make of it?" he asked the surgeon. "What can all these clocks and dials mean? And what about this thing that looks like a piano?"

"My poor friend, I haven't the vaguest idea! If we are indeed inside a balloon, it may be part of the machinery, but what could its function be?"

"I'd give a lot to know. *Sacrénom!* I'm beginning to be sorry that we ever set foot in this devilish contraption."

"Look at this," said Bourief, who was rummaging around the room. "This strange picture with two globes on it...."

Both officers came over and saw a little screen on which were two spheres against a jet-black background. The first, bluish with coils of white on its surface, looked like a lapis-lazuli child's marble of considerable size, but they could make nothing of it. As they watched, it grew smaller and the second one grew larger.

Then Faultrier, who was scrutinizing the screen with attention, said in a voice strangled by emotion: "Why, that looks like the moon, damn it!"

"What are you raving about?" grumbled Bernard. "The moon? With all those holes in it it looks more like a Swiss cheese!"

"I'd bet my life on it, I'm so sure! While I was a student in Paris I often amused myself by watching the

33

moon through a telescope. . . . We're climbing toward it, and at one hell of a speed!"

"If that's true, then the other globe must be . . ."

". . . The Earth. Great balls of fire! This damn balloon has lifted off!"

The captain was paralyzed for a moment as he tried to comprehend the situation. After a few seconds he got a grip on himself.

"You must be out of your mind! It would be impossible to climb that high in a balloon—unless the devil himself had built the thing. The scene must be a trompe l'oeil like the others. Look. Watch this."

His bayonet at the ready, the captain charged into one of the huge bays that represented a mountain scene, and with all his force he dug the pointed blade into the protective shield.

The result was immediate: a tremendous implosion that tossed him head over heels, while a plastic film swelled out, retaining the various bits of debris, and then settled back into place again. Instead of the picturesque view of the mountain, there was now only a dark rectangle with a few twisted wires.

"There, you can see for yourself," groaned the officer, getting to his feet. "There's nothing behind these pictures. It's all only an illusion. The same must be true of the other. We haven't budged from the ground, and I'll bet that somebody wants to frighten us. Bah! If we just keep trying, we'll find some way out of this contraption."

Faultrier seemed unconvinced. He continued to watch the little screen on which the Earth was getting smaller and smaller each second. The moon itself had been left behind. The surgeon had been able to see the craters, the mountain chains; he would have sworn he had recognized the characteristic contours of Copernicus. Other objects then drew his attention. He began recognizing the planets of the solar system.

The machine they were in must have been moving at an incredible speed, because already the pale disk of the moon was minute. On the other hand, the surgeon could clearly recognize Jupiter, with its characteristic bands, and farther on, Saturn and its ring.

"You know," he began, "I don't really understand how, but I'm convinced that we have . . ."

He never finished his sentence. The captain, who was moving nervously around the room, had just pressed one of the keys of the "piano," and what happened next made Faultrier think that he had gone out of his mind.

All sensation of weight had disappeared. Bernard, his finger still pressing the key, had his feet in the air and his head pointing down. The others tried to come to his rescue, but, alas, they all started to fly around the room in the strangest postures.

The soldiers swore like fifty devils, while the Russian women squealed and vainly tried to hold down their floating skirts.

Rifles, shakos, pistols, circled around gracefully, banging into the walls or floor and then smartly bouncing off again in the opposite direction.

"The swine have bewitched us!" shouted Bernard. "Look at me walking along the ceiling as though I were a fly."

"It's not possible!" moaned Chastel. "I must be as drunk as a lord. The captain is flying around like a bird!"

"For once in my life I think I must have overeaten," groaned Bourief. "My stomach's playing tricks on me."

"*Kurva!*" Kaninski bawled furiously, kicking out in all directions and trying to latch on to one of the Russian women. "Bunch of sluts! You've thrown a spell over us! But I swear on my honor as a hussar that you're not going to get away with it. If I get my hands on you . . ."

Only Faultrier remained relatively lucid. Once the first shock of surprise was over, he decided to apply Descartes' experimental method to the situation and noticed that by making judiciously calculated motions he could propel himself in any desired direction. He therefore waited until he had reached the ceiling, and pushing against it with his hand he propelled himself to where he could seize the bottom of Bernard's pants.

The captain in turn held on to him with an energy born of despair and grunted, "My God, do you have any idea of what's going on?"

"Not much, damn it. It almost seems as though we have suddenly become weightless."

"You can't mean that! How do we get back to normal?"

"Maybe if we could press down again on that piano key you touched just a moment ago . . ."

"That's fine with me, but the devil take it if I can remember which of them it was."

"Try to calm down and remember," suggested the surgeon as he made them glide directly over their goal—though perhaps at a faster speed then he would have liked.

His hand clutching at the instrument, his forehead dripping sweat, the captain struggled to reassemble his thoughts.

While this was going on, the soldiers continued on their merry rounds. They were a little calmer by now, and even beginning to take a certain pleasure in this unusual situation.

"It was that one," Bernard said finally, pointing to a yellow key.

"Are you sure?"

"Yes, I remember very clearly now. I was thinking that it was almost the same color as the buttons on your jacket."

"Well, then, go to it. No matter what happens, I don't see that we've anything to lose, given our present situation. . . ."

The officer's finger hesitated over the key and then pressed down with fierce determination.

Everything immediately returned to normal—with all due allowance, that is, for the fact that since the occupants of the room were in no way prepared, their contact with the ground was rather sudden and sharp.

"*Saprelotte!*" ejaculated Bernard, pulling a handkerchief from his pocket and mopping his forehead. "Faultrier, you really know how to keep your head. As for myself, I've never had such a scare—not even at Jena, when the bullets were flying over my head. Everything seems normal now. If anybody touches anything, I'll skin him alive!"

"We're back to where we were a little while ago," remarked Faultrier, sounding disappointed, "but that doesn't mean we're out of this mess. If you ask me, old friend, I'm convinced that our balloon has taken off, and that we've left the Earth behind."

This time the captain offered no objections. The minutes he had just lived through had forever erased from his mind the image of a well-ordered universe in which the sun came up every morning and in which apples fell downward as they were supposed to do. Ready to believe anything, he grumbled:

"Damn it, you're probably right! I'm an old campaigner, and I've seen a lot in my life. Until now, I've always managed to work things out to my advantage, and there's no reason why I shouldn't be able to this time! By God, I'll get the best of this situation before it's over! Fix bayonets and follow me! There must be somebody hidden on this diabolical mechanism! When I lay my hands on the wretches, I can promise you they'll see what a French officer is made of!"

The soldiers quick-stepped completely around the level they were on, but they found no one. They then returned to the central shaft, where Faultrier made an extremely interesting discovery.

Accidentally placing his hand on the edge of the vertical cylinder, he had the impression that it was being drawn upward. The captain then experimented, first with a piece of gun waste, then with a bit of wood, and finally with a bullet; he saw that all these objects were immediately drawn toward the upper floors of the balloon. On the other hand, when a cartridge was bounced against the wall it began to rise, but once it had reached the center of the shaft it came down again.

"There seems to be no doubt that everything happens as though there were a strong current of air pushing things to the ceiling when they are next to the walls," remarked the doctor.

"Well, we'll soon find out," declared the captain. "The damned jokesters who have played these tricks on us must be on the upper floors. Follow me!"

Without a moment's hesitation, Bernard entered the shaft and, as had been foreseen, smoothly began to rise, followed by his little troop.

They left the shaft on the level immediately over the one from which they came. The layout was similar: a central axis surrounded by eight triangular rooms. They seemed to be storerooms crammed with a various assortment of cases and boxes.

Without wasting any more time, Bernard mounted to the next level. This time they found curious vehicles, similar to hermetically sealed carriages. Strange armor with transparent visors hung from the walls. Oddly enough, some of the armor had six and even eight arm and leg pieces. As for the gauntlets, they were of a great variety of forms.

On orders from their captain, the men were careful not to touch a thing, and they all mounted to the next level.

The first rooms here seemed filled with unidentifiable weapons—elongated tubes, brilliant spirals, hooked antennas—that were inspected with great care. Then they opened the next door, following the procedure Svetlana had discovered, and this time a cry of surprise escaped from the throats of the two officers.

Supine on the floor before them were some ten nightmarish creatures—a brood of demons—with clawlike feet at the end of metallic coils, arms terminated by six pincers that simulated fingers, and the whole crowned by a globular head with three eyes on protruding stalks, absolutely rigid hair, and two funnel-shaped horns where ears should be.

Bernard and his men, who were not what might be described as regular churchgoers or true believers, mechanically crossed themselves. Faultrier was the only one who dared enter the room and touch one of the misshapen beings with the tip of his saber. He noticed that the limbs of the creature were moving feebly and that its ocelli were fixed on him.

Gathering courage, Faultrier continued his investigation and came to one of these mysterious creatures lying near an instrument that was similar to the piano below. He had a flexible nozzle in his paws and seemed to be trying to adjust it to a hole in his slender thorax.

The surgeon bent over and easily slid the nozzle in. At that point he was joined by Bernard.

"Do you think these grotesque monsters are alive?" asked the captain.

"I think so," answered his friend. "I'm even convinced that they are the masters of this balloon, but that for some reason or other they have been immobilized."

"Sick?"

"Perhaps paralyzed. They move, but only very weakly."

"I don't like the look of any of this! Maybe we should slice them up before they get a chance to play any tricks on us!"

"Get a grip on yourself. For the moment there's no reason to think that they're anything but inoffensive creatures. If they make you nervous, why don't you have them tied?"

"You're right. It's best to be careful." And addressing the soldiers, he added: "All right, men, let's get these phenomena properly trussed up!"

While Friancourt went off to search for harness reins with which to carry out his chief's orders, the other troopers, sabers drawn, remained on the alert, ready for anything. Or at least, that's what they thought.

The creature whose nozzle Faultrier had adjusted was rapidly returning to life. The little stems on its head were whirling, and its ocelli were staring at the men before it.

"Look," remarked Bernard. "That one seems to be moving. . . ."

They turned toward the misshapen creature, and to their surprise it got up on its metal feet with a disconcerting agility and rushed to the nearby piano. Its fingers touched several keys. At that very instant the captain raised his pistol and was squeezing the trigger.

But the officer was unable to complete his movement, for suddenly all the humans in the room were simultaneously paralyzed.

Chapter Four

Incapable of lifting so much as a pinky, but perfectly conscious, they saw the grotesque creature raise his kindred one after another and lead them to the nozzle which he connected to the intake on their thorax.

After a few seconds with the nozzle inserted, each creature seemed sufficiently recovered to stand up on his own. Curiously enough, none of them paid any attention to the humans, who stood there like so many wax statues. Instead, they gathered around the keyboard and attentively inspected the various dials, without exchanging the least word.

Then, after endless minutes, several of the monsters went off, after first arming themselves with what seemed like pistols with transparent butts.

It was only then that the creature who had been the first to stir, thereby surprising the soldiers, decided to pay some attention to his prisoners.

He rummaged through a cabinet and took out several tubes terminating in small suction cups, then a filmy fabric resembling a hairnet from which dangled some metallic excrescences.

Lifting Faultrier by the waist, he carried him over to this curious apparatus, attached the suction cups to his hands and throat, and placed the hairnet on his head.

The transparent tubes immediately filled with blood, a minuscule scalpel cut clean into a few millimeters of the skin covering the thumb, and the specimen was placed in the machine.

For the next five minutes the surgeon's torturer stood there immobile, as though listening to a voice inaudible to the Earthlings. Then he carefully detached the suction cups and left only the net in place.

Faultrier began to have an extraordinary sensation: though he didn't hear a word, it seemed as if somebody were speaking to him—and what he thought he understood made him doubt his sanity.

"Well, my friend, you almost made a real mess of things! Luckily you connected my iono-sterilizing regenerator, otherwise this ship would have smashed right into a star! In any case, we are out of danger now. I owe you a few explanations, though I doubt that your primitive brain will be capable of understanding what I am about to say. To begin with, allow me to introduce myself: my name is Ar'zog and I'm a Fortrun from a far-off planet in the Eridanus constellation. An unforeseen incident caused us to become paralyzed after landing on your planet. It was really quite silly. We had to fill our reservoirs with your air, which analysis had shown corresponded to our needs. Our computer—a machine that works for us and often even thinks for us—had tested its chemical and bacteriological properties. But I'm forgetting that you don't have any idea of what I'm talking about! Let's just say that the computer had tested it to make sure that its composition was suitable for us and that it contained nothing that would make us sick. But by an unusual stroke of bad luck, a tiny part of our computer had deteriorated after exposure to invisible rays that we call cosmic. As a result, the computer did what was necessary to destroy the large and fatal disease germs, but not the small ones— those that we call viruses. . . . Oh, how difficult it is to explain anything to someone as backward as you are! Never mind, I suppose that several sessions with the oniro-educator will teach you a few basics. In short, as soon as we breathed your air we became sick: an almost total paralysis prevented us from moving. That's why you were able to enter the ship and do so many idiotic things, whereas we had been able to drive off the first intruders. Have you understood any of this? Just think your questions, and I will reply. . . ."

Faultrier desperately tried to get his ideas in order. Everything seemed to be happening with the implacable logic of a nightmare. And yet he was convinced that he was not dreaming: the recent feast with the Russian women inside this diabolical contraption was very real; his stomach was no longer aching with hunger. Obviously, this fantastic story of extraterrestrials who had arrived on a vessel that could navigate between the stars was somewhat stupefying, but the memory of the Earth disappearing on the small screen, the passage close to the moon, the familiar planets of the solar system, all corroborated the tale of this mechanical aberration who could express himself without speaking! He therefore thought:

"What you've just told me is a bit beyond my ability to understand: several things seem incomprehensible to me. For instance, your body looks like metal. Is it living material?"

"Ah! A judicious question. It shows that in spite of your scientific ignorance your intelligence quotient is rather high, and this makes me hopeful. But to get back to your question. I must confess that we Fortruns have kept only the brain of our original body. Try to understand: by transplanting the encephalon into a sealed compartment irrigated by blood, we avoid all the disease and suffering linked to that imperfect machine, that envelope of flesh to which you are still riveted. A pump circulates our blood, and compressed air in a storage chamber gives us great respiratory autonomy—about a ten-day supply. But don't think that we are isolated from the outside world! Our sensory centers are linked to delicate mechanisms that transmit sights and sounds to us with a sensitivity that you cannot begin to imagine. Protected in this way against exterior forces, we live for hundreds of years without falling sick. Only the unfortunate accident to our computer exposed us to illness. Because of what I've told you, we are vigorous and healthy and can enjoy life without fear."

"Enjoy life?" asked the surgeon in amazement. "Imprisoned as you are in a metal body?"

"That may seem strange to a primitive like yourself," admitted the Fortrun indulgently. "But just think about it a minute: we can stimulate our nerve ends in any way we want, and thus simulate every imaginable pleasure! It is true that this ability is not without danger, and present events prove it. The Fortruns have become a race of sybarites almost completely preoccupied with enjoying life. We have a vast empire, our planets are rich in metals of all kinds, our fleet is large, and nevertheless we have come to ask your help. . . ."

"How can that be?" Faultrier asked in bewilderment. "If you are as highly evolved as you say, how can primitive beings like ourselves be of any use to you?"

"Let me explain," said Ar'zog with some embarrassment. "An enemy race has recently appeared on our frontiers. They are the Kveyars, a dynamic people who have just attained to a galactic level of civilization by developing rapid and well-armed ships capable of traveling great distances."

"If you have warships, why haven't you driven them off?"

"The reason's very simple. For centuries my people have lived in peace and have therefore completely forgotten the arts of war. Without proper programming, our computers are of no use to us. On several occasions airfleets directed by them have been utterly destroyed by the Kveyars. Since these demons give us no respite, we have to take fast action. Our computers have therefore advised that we search among the inhabited planets for a people who seem trained in the art of combat. Test observations show that your kind have a great deal of experience in this domain. And that is why we have come to look for a few individuals on Earth—in order to make them our military leaders."

"And what makes you think that we will be willing to accept this role?" the surgeon asked in some surprise. "I've spent my life caring for wounded men, and I've had my fill of this sort of entertainment."

"It's not you but your companions that we are interested in," Ar'zog replied reassuringly. "We are going to take advantage of our time en route home to give you an oniro-pedagogic treatment that will provide you with the necessary scientific understanding."

"You must be completely mad! There are only eight of us, six enlisted men, myself, and one officer. . . ."

"What about the females who are with you?"

"They have absolutely no military training. In order to direct your fleets, we would need a cadre ten times as large."

"Don't worry about that. We will take care of these details, and even your cherished horses will be the object of all our care."

"Ar'zog, I beg of you, listen to me a moment. There is something you don't seem to understand. We are primitive beings, and your scientific achievements are completely beyond us. I myself have always been interested in technical progress, and so can make some effort to understand what you tell me. My companions, however, have absolutely no idea of what the stars really are. They think we're in a balloon that's floating over the Earth. Even if you get them to admit that it's possible to navigate the immeasurable distances between the stars, they'll never agree to leave their homeland forever! This backward planet is ours! We need its sun, its vast plains, its trees and rivers. Nothing can replace them for us. Come, be sensible. Nothing irreparable has been done. They don't know what has happened. Take us back to where you found us. By all that I hold most sacred, I promise never to tell anybody what I have just learned. In any case, you needn't worry—nobody would ever believe me!"

The Fortrun appeared moved by this pathetic appeal, for he hesitated a moment before replying:

"I am quite aware of the problems entailed in this kidnapping. We have deliberately broken a cosmic law that forbids all interference in the affairs of peoples who have not yet achieved sufficient psychic and technological maturity. However, the very existence of our civilization is at stake. Only you—backward savages with all your bellicose instincts still intact—can save us. The Kveyars are shamelessly pillaging and sacking our peaceful empire, and things cannot go this way. Given the stakes, the fate of a few individuals doesn't matter. You have been chosen by destiny for a new existence that will tear you from the banality of an Earthbound life and launch you into space at the head of powerful fleets! In a few hours you have leaped over the gulf of centuries and learned what your retarded compatriots will not learn until much later—provided that they don't kill each other off before then. It has been our experience that civilizations made up of warlike races are often destroyed when they manage to harness the power of the atom! But let's not discuss that, since you cannot possibly understand. I would like you to know that this conversation will not have been in vain, as I will take it into account when I program my oniro-suggesters to instill in you the desire to navigate through space. You will soon forget your bluish planet—which I must admit seems reasonably pleasant, at least in its temperate regions."

Faultrier wanted to continue pleading his cause, but the contact between them was broken. As if in a dream, he saw several Fortruns grab hold of his still inert companions and place them in cubicles. After having stretched them out on long, vertically inclined tables, they fixed wires to their foreheads with the aid of suction cups and then closed the transparent doors on them. The peasant women, who had been seized and similarly paralyzed by the extraterrestrial weapons, met the same fate. Finally, Faultrier, carried in the careful claws of Ar'zog, whose globular eyes remained fixed on him reassuringly, was in turn placed in a similar cubicle.

"Don't be afraid, my friend," he understood before sinking into unconsciousness. "You are in no danger. When you wake up, everything will seem considerably more simple."

For ten days—as time is measured on Earth—the Fortrun spaceship sped toward Epsilon Eridani. The soldiers and the Russian women reposed peacefully in their cubicles. As for the horses, they had been placed in great plastic sacks and left to hibernate, because the extraterrestrials really didn't know what to do with these strange animals. As a matter of course, they had also submitted the horses to a psycho-stimulant treatment, curious to see what would be the outcome of the experiment. During their various voyages the Fortruns had come across quadrupeds of this kind who had a reasonably developed intelligence and a great deal of wisdom, though they seemed uninterested in scientific progress. . . .

A few hours before landing, Ar'zog and his companions decided to interrupt the treatment the Earthlings were undergoing. The oniro-educators had accomplished their task and the Fortruns were eager to see the reactions of those from whom they expected salvation.

The soldiers were therefore taken from the narrow compartments in which they had made the voyage and comfortably installed in pneumatic armchairs, where they very quickly regained consciousness.

"*Sacaristi!*" Bernard groaned as he stretched his arms. "That was a good snooze. I haven't felt this relaxed in a long time!"

"You're right," agreed Faultrier. "We all needed that. Say," he continued, "there's Ar'zog! Those gadgets of yours are fantastic. You don't feel a blessed thing. How long were we under treatment?"

"About ten of your days. . . ."

"I'd swear I haven't slept more than a night!" exclaimed the captain. "And yet I know that what you say is true. Those oniro-educators are sensational. I feel as though I've learned heaps of things about which I hadn't the slightest inkling. And this way of talking by merely thinking is really very practical!"

"You seem to have correctly assimilated the telepsychic process, and I'm very pleased. . . ."

The Fortrun remained reserved; he was waiting for some reaction from his new allies to the propositions that had been made to them while they slept. Bernard didn't keep him waiting long.

"Let's get down to cases," continued the captain, feeling very sure of himself. "If I'm to believe what your machines have told me while I was asleep, you have need of mercenaries to combat the Kveyars. You've tricked us as though we were children. But never mind that now. Here we are, dragged into an interstellar conflict against our wills! I would never have believed anything like this, even in my wildest dreams! Alas, I'm afraid that your inexperience in military matters has led you to commit an error. . . . If I have understood correctly, you want me to take over your fleets and use my men as subalterns, right?"

"Exactly."

"Well, Ar'zog, my friend, you should have captured an admiral and some navy officers! Space combat strikes me as being closer to naval strategy than to ground maneuvers."

"Our computers were aware of this point. Let me explain why we preferred to make use of your services. For many years now your countrymen have been fighting against coalitions of nations, and you have acquired an extraordinary amount of experience that has resulted in numerous victories. On the seas, however, your admirals have not been very lucky. We could, of course, have invited some English sailors in your place, but actually, they have had only limited occasions to put their tactical theories into practice, and the results, although spectacular, have not struck us as very conclusive. At the Battle of Trafalgar, for example, the state of your ships and the disparity of the Spanish and French crews gave your Admiral Villeneuve no opportunity at all. Surcouf might have tempted us, but he is much too famous and his disappearance could have modified the course of your history; we couldn't allow that. On the other hand, who would notice your disappearance? Innumerable officers and enlisted men are going to freeze to death on the Russian steppes, and a few corpses more or less won't matter. Your service records seem quite satisfactory to us. You were attached to imperial headquarters during the 1805 campaigns and during Austerlitz—a model of strategy, if I'm to believe your memories of the occasion. . . . We are counting on you to give the men under you the necessary training.

Oniro-educators will be placed at your disposal. And since your little group contains men experienced in the use of almost all the types of weapons used in your wars, we are assured of having at our disposition the elements necessary to provide a cadre for our armed forces."

"Fine, then! It would be foolish of me to be more demanding than you are. Nevertheless, before I agree, I have to clear up a number of points. To begin with, for myself I demand absolute authority over all military operations. When I decide to make such and such a move, I will expect to carry it out with the means and arms that I alone decide are necessary and appropriate. My orders are in no case to be disputed. Is that understood?"

Ar'zog meditated a moment. He consulted the shipboard computer by means of the keyboard and then replied:

"Of course. You are the only competent authority. Nevertheless, in case of repeated failure, we reserve the right to dismiss you from your command."

"I accept. Another thing. Logically, a simple captain cannot command such a great number of squadrons. I therefore demand the rank of general, Commander in Chief of the Fortrun Armed Forces. In addition, I want to have the right to promote my men to such ranks as I feel correspond to the services they render."

"If it amuses you. I see no reason to object. Until now, these titles have not existed among us. However, we are quite aware that such practices are current in your country."

"Fine. I would also like to have the power to dispense titles of nobility once a planet has been delivered from the enemy yoke and placed under the jurisdiction of myself or one of my men."

The Fortrun once more consulted his mentor, who this time seemed a little hesitant.

"Before replying, I have to ask for some details. This local ruler—will he in the final analysis obey the laws that are in force in our empire and established by our central computer?"

"Obviously, he will not break them unless the military situation makes it necessary, and in such a case he will be responsible to me and to you as leader of the central authority established on your planet."

"In which case, we accept."

Bernard seemed satisfied. He had always had great ambitions, and circumstances had not made it possible for him to rise through the ranks of the hierarchy as quickly as he would have liked. This adventure opened undreamed-of perspectives to him. He therefore decided to make further demands.

"Now let's talk a little about the question of bonuses and such. If all goes well and the Kveyars are driven from your possessions, I am sure that you will show yourselves generous. I demand that when our job is done we be allowed to return to our own planet."

"Of course. You understand, however, that it will then be necessary to erase from your minds the memories of the events you have lived through."

The French officer nodded in agreement.

"That's obvious. In any case, nobody would believe us! But let's get back to practical matters. I demand that every Earth month each of my men receive an ingot of pure gold, no matter what the results of the fighting, and that I get double that."

Ar'zog seemed amused by this request.

"Agreed! But I thought you understood that this metal has no particular value in our country. Our mines are filled with it and we can synthesize it at will. Every Fortrun citizen can have all the comfort he would like, and in cases where he needs special equipment—a spaceship, for example—his request is examined by our computers and granted if it corresponds to a real need."

"I know, but that won't protect our old age if we decide to return to Earth. In addition, I reserve for myself a part of the war booty—a hundredth of the precious stones and metals taken."

"Trifles! Is that all?"

"Yes. This agreement is to be set down in a document which we will both sign in order to assure that our respective engagements are carried out. As soon as this is done, I will be at your disposition to commence the training of the men under me. That will no doubt take several weeks. Our limited manpower makes this something of a problem. Frankly, if we had ten times our number I would feel more optimistic about this project. I've very little confidence in your robots and electronic brains being able to make correct decisions in the heat of battle!"

"This point has also been foreseen, and I'll explain the solution we arrived at as soon as we have landed on my planet. We will supply you with arms and ships with which to begin the training of your men, because every minute counts. There is not a second to lose."

"You can count on me. I'll get to work immediately."

On the shipboard screens an amethyst ball was rapidly increasing in size. Panel lights kept going off and on. The computer replied to requests for identification and made contact with the beacon satellites for landing maneuvers.

Faultrier, who until then had remained silent, now intervened energetically.

"All this is very well, but you seem to be forgetting one small thing, my dear Bernard. In your haste to begin massacring people who have done you no harm, you have forgotten about me! I have not the slightest intention of letting you down, however, and I want to be in a position to care for those of us who are wounded. You'll have to see to it that I have the equipment I need. Géraudont will assist me."

"These feelings do you honor," said Ar'zog. "Your compatriots are indeed capable people, but they are also bloodthirsty brutes who rather frighten me. You will be given everything you want and even more, since you will be initiated into our techniques and they are sure to amaze you—especially in the domain of prosthetic replacement. Operating rooms and specialized robots will be placed at your disposal."

"Good. That makes me feel better. I'm eager to get to work, because what I've learned while I was sleeping has been simply astonishing. I hope to put my new skills into practice."

"You see, everything is working out!" said Bernard with a hearty laugh. "And to inaugurate my new powers I hereby name you Chief Surgeon of the Fortrun Army. Try to find a suitable uniform as soon as we arrive."

Chapter Five

Aware of his new responsibilities and of the fact that he represented the Imperial Army in the galaxy, General Bernard carried out a close inspection of his small troop before they disembarked at the military astroport of Dumyat, the Fortrun capital.

Rips in cloaks had been repaired as well as possible, uniforms were cleaned, weapons waxed, and shoes polished. Every trooper always carried the necessary material for these operations in his knapsack.

The saddles had been scrubbed, and the horses curry-combed. In some extraordinary way the horses seemed to understand the intentions of their masters: reins were almost unnecessary in guiding them.

Spurs, too, had become superfluous. On the other hand, the horses seemed to have developed very definite ideas of their prerogatives and would allow themselves to be mounted only by their masters.

Despite minor irritations, and despite a squabble between Bourief and Lisa, who absolutely insisted on sitting behind him in the saddle for the parade that was to follow the landing—a posture that would have been considered extremely unmilitary in every army in the world—Bernard declared himself satisfied with the appearance of his men.

When the troopers, perched on their mounts, rode through the air locks, they looked quite splendid. However, they were extremely disappointed by what they saw: they had expected a warm welcome with fanfares and flags, but instead they found only a vast, almost deserted esplanade, with only a few robots who were responsible for the unloading of the spaceships;

53

the passengers of the vertical takeoff mechanisms that were landing on every side paid them no attention.

Ar'zog eventually took them in charge and politely led the way to a jet-shuttle in which they took seats. The ship immediately gained altitude and carried the soldiers to the quarters that had been reserved for them.

The spectacle they saw from the large portholes soon made them forget their disappointment: the Fortruns had made their planet into a veritable Paradise.

With the exception of the astroport installations, there were no buildings on ground level. All the energy centers and factories were deep in the earth. As far as the eye could see, there were vast plains with scattered clumps of trees that sported purplish-blue leaves. Waterways lazily insinuated themselves across the landscape, and on their banks birds with multicolored plumage flew about fearlessly.

The flora and fauna had been domesticated for centuries. Science had made it possible to select the species that were most agreeable to the eye. Innumerable flowers speckled the meadows, and their colorful corollas equaled the beauty of the most sumptuous orchids.

The climate, completely controlled by satellites that regulated rainfall, offered no unpleasant surprises. Immense mirrors orbiting the planet made it possible to heat the atmosphere during the winter, while in the summer the controlled melting of polar glaciers brought to the shorelines icy currents that lowered the temperature.

The Fortruns, amiable sybarites that they were, had no fixed domiciles. Mobile habitations made it possible to move from spot to spot and continent to continent pretty much as they pleased. Every comfort they desired was available to them. Each house was provided with a perfect system of color-smell-relief television whose giant cubic screen occupied the center of the main room.

The transparent sides of the globe that sheltered their living quarters made it possible to enjoy the landscape.

During the night a continuous aurora borealis spread its luminescent waves.

Every home had, of course, an oniro-suggester, which made it possible to experience at will the pleasures of the most subtle artificial paradises.

Sometimes, on nights illuminated by the satellites, the Fortruns would gather in the midst of a vast clearing. There, in psychic communion, they would be filled with ecstatic joy by an omnisensory symphony.

Few of them had regular duties to perform. Some painted or sculpted, others devoted themselves to the sciences; nobody exhausted himself by hard labor. The computers took care of the planning, the robots of the work.

Habituated to this idyllic life, the Fortruns could not even conceive of the possibility of employing violence, much less of going to war. The aggression of the Kveyars had surprised them like a sudden clap of thunder in a calm sky. Luckily for them, a few astronauts such as their leader Ar'zog, who often navigated from star to star, still had some rudiments of common sense. Upon the advice of the computers, the council of notables had agreed to allow Ar'zog to search out a place where there would be mercenaries capable of defending them: he decided on the planet Earth, which was bloodied by endless wars.

The Earthlings each received a globe-house, but since they were little used to living on dreams, time lay heavily on their hands. Tania and Bernard and Katia and Faultrier soon formed couples, and the others paired off as best they could.

The horses were left free to roam in the neighboring meadows. Vaccinated as their masters had been against all the microbes on the planet—this time the computers had overlooked nothing—they greedily nibbled at the thick grass, which seemed to suit them just fine.

The Earthlings received their food from a robot-domestic who was programmed to cater to their tastes by dishing up caviar, sauerkraut, or beef stew. Of course, these preparations were actually cleverly compounded synthetics, but nobody complained.

The faucets even distributed an alcoholic drink that had the brownish color of Cinzano, was aromatic, pleasing to the palate, and even when overindulged in had no disagreeable morning-after effects.

As soon as he had settled in, Bernard, without ignoring the gentle pleasures of that marvelous planet, set to work with a will.

He began by inquiring into the armaments placed by the Fortruns at his disposal. The commercial fleet was large: more than five hundred well-equipped and rapid ships. However, none of them had arms that were worth the name. They had anti-meteorite screens and light-weight disintegrators—more efficient than four- or twelve-piece artillery batteries on Earth, but laughable when compared with what the Kveyars had equipped their invasion fleet.

To his great amazement, the new general learned that the Fortruns had supplies of a number of fearsome arms: antimatter missiles, space distorters, and even mechanisms that could take their spaceships out of the time-phase and thus make them invisible. But these idlers, much too preoccupied with the pleasures of life, had never developed weapons production lest the subsequent drain on energy force them to reduce their standard of living. They had merely sent up some hastily equipped spaceships manned by robots, and of course their adversaries had easily destroyed them.

Bernard soon decided it would not be too difficult to equip the existing vessels so that they could fight off the Kveyars without the vast Fortrun empire becoming economically unbalanced. After all, the Fortruns still controlled more than a hundred planets, and only some ten of these were being threatened at this time.

Ar'zog immediately recognized the need to change the present state of affairs, and without pushing for the construction of new ships, he received from the computers permission to arm all available vessels in a suitable manner.

Reassured on this point, Bernard immediately worked out a short-term plan of action designed to slow the progress of the Kveyars by showing the will to resist of those they considered soft, sensuous, and contemptible beings—epicureans incapable of confronting the horrors of war. Until now the Fortruns had not done anything to try to liberate the planetary systems occupied by the invader.

The Kveyars often merely disembarked on a planet and looted it, taking great care not to destroy the factories and mines which they could make profitable use of. After leaving a small garrison behind, they would push on. All attempts at resistance were pitilessly repressed by the most cruel means.

As a result, the power of the Kveyars increased with each passing day. The resources of their new conquests allowed them to build as many ships as they wanted. On their home planet they had had to submit to draconian rationing because of the scarcity of certain metals, especially radioactive ores.

So as not to lose time and also to familiarize his men with the weapons they would have available to them, Bernard asked that a special zone be set aside as a testing range. Ar'zog seemed somewhat reluctant to do this and suggested that these tests be carried out on an asteroid, but the general did not care to shuttle back and forth endlessly and so he refused point-blank. He was therefore given his way: an area some hundred kilometers square was marked off and closed to all unauthorized persons.

The mercenaries were overjoyed at this decision. The inactivity was beginning to bore them. Although each of them had set up housekeeping with one of the Russian women—to the great satisfaction of all—and none was eager to be separated from his beloved in the near future.

The globe-houses were transported to the periphery of the weapons range, and every man settled down to train with the arms that corresponded to his specialty.

As artillery men, Bourief and Chastel took charge of the heavy disintegrators paired with cone-shaped, teleguided nuclear missiles. Mounted on antigrav platforms, these weapons could rapidly be moved over all types of terrain. The disintegrators had a range of only about a kilometer. The missiles, however, could unerringly hit targets beyond the horizon. Equipped with mimetic screens that took on the coloring of the surrounding landscape, these mechanisms were extremely difficult to spot, even with radar, because of their antireflective sheathing.

Once they had fired off a few shots, the two gunners fell in love with these little gems and regretted not having had access to them when they were fighting on the Russian steppes. ...

While this was going on, Queunot, Kaninski, and Friancourt were having contests with light arms, each more marvelous than the next. Actually, the men were demonstrating very little personal skill in massacring the peaceful woodland creatures, for the infrared-guided californium bullets sped right to any target emitting heat. When the unhappy Ar'zog saw the carnage and came across the bloody and torn animal corpses, he all but fainted; obviously the mores of these primitives were unbelievably cruel. He made no attempt to interfere, but he did take a mental vow never again to check on the skill of his mercenaries—especially since after these exercises the bloodthirsty Earthlings would also treat themselves to the luxury of hunting down inoffensive grazing animals with their archaic rifles, butchering them, and roasting the sides of meat over a wood fire. ...

Bernard was completely happy with the adaptability of his men, who had perfectly assimilated the new elements inherent in these perfected weapons. He therefore next decided to train them to use robots as shock troops so that they would not have to expose their own lives in the coming engagements. The metal creatures furnished by the Fortruns obeyed the psychically issued orders of the Earthlings, parading in an impeccable manner, taking up firing positions, or launching an attack by zigzagging under the simulated fire of an enemy whose arms were as murderous as their own. Of course, the anti-g with which the robots had been equipped made possible trajectories that were inconceivable with conventional troops on Earth. ...

Three companies of one hundred robots each had soon been trained in all the ruses of war; they were supported by two artillery groups ready for rapid intervention on every sort of terrain.

Bernard declared himself satisfied with these preliminary results, and one evening as he puffed away at his pipe he expanded on his plans to Faultrier.

"This tobacco is not bad," he began, "but still, it lacks a little something."

"You're just being difficult," protested his friend. "Actually, you ought to be thanking me, for without my help you would never have had any tobacco at all! The synthesizers refused to produce such a noxious drug, containing highly toxic alkaloids and producing carcinogenic hydrocarbons as it burns. I had to insist by saying that we needed it to stimulate our intelligence."

"Bah!" said the officer as he swatted at the well-rounded buttocks of Tania, who happened to be passing within range. "I'm not complaining. The food is acceptable, and these Russian ladies are lively enough. In the final analysis, I'm not sorry to have switched planets— we've learned a great deal that we didn't know anything about."

"There's one thing I can't get used to: our horses have become so stubbornly independent. It's as if they have their own ideas about what has to be done."

"I admit they're getting difficult to handle. It must be the fault of the psycho-stimulating treatment."

"You know, I've seen some extraordinary things in the Fortrun biological centers. These people are fantastic."

"Yes, they certainly know how to live! Their music is pleasant, and I've experimented with a few drugs that I had never heard about. As for their oniro-suggesters— terrific. . . ."

"You wouldn't be letting the delights of Dumyat soften you up, would you? I don't notice any special hurry on your part to confront these damned Kveyars, and Ar'zog is not going to be at all happy about that! Especially since he's kept his part of the bargain: we've received those gold ingots right on schedule."

"Don't worry your head over it. Of course I'm profiting from the advantages of life in a rear echelon, but that doesn't mean I haven't been mulling over our mission. Actually, I wanted to discuss my plans with you."

"Ah! There's the restless, bloodthirsty Bernard I know! Go on, I'm listening."

And so saying, the doctor poured himself a glass of wine, which he sipped at, then clacked his tongue in satisfaction and settled back into his armchair.

"Here's how things stand: I can't launch a large-scale offensive with the troops available to me at present. I've therefore been thinking about a limited action on one of the planets occupied by the Kveyars at the beginning of their offensive. According to what I've learned from the computers, the garrison there isn't very large. Besides, given their methods of repression, they don't feel they have anything to fear from the occupied peoples. Oloch, the target I'm thinking of, doesn't have a natural satellite. The fort which commands access to the Kveyar base is at the top of a mountain surrounded by an all but impenetrable marsh—according to the Fortruns. But you know what these Fortruns are like. In spite of their mechanical bodies, they hate to be uncomfortable, and the idea of marching for several hours and then having to sleep outdoors is just unthinkable to them."

"I see what you're getting at. The Kveyars are only on guard over the aerial approaches, and an attack coming from the marshes would take them completely by surprise!"

"Exactly! Especially since the heavy vegetation would provide perfect cover for our approach. If we do this, we can form a better idea of the capacities of our enemies so that we will know their weak points and be able to fight against them more efficiently in the future."

"You've obviously lost nothing of your enthusiasm

for war! The idea has possibilities, but I think we can get more out of it than you've suggested."

"Really? Let's hear what you've got in mind."

"Well, if you could capture Oloch without giving its garrison time to call for help, you would considerably increase the value of such a surprise attack. The Kveyars don't know that we're here. The sudden disappearance of their garrison would worry them enormously, and since the Fortruns are incapable of pulling off such a stunt, the Kveyars would go out of their minds wondering who was attacking them. They won't at all like this business of being hit from the rear, and while they're trying to figure things out, they'll have to call a halt to their offensive. That will give you additional time in which to increase your forces, and time is on our side. Every day more and more ships are being armed."

Bernard was delighted with the plan. Bringing his fist down on the table before him, he made the glasses on it dance.

"Sheer genius! I will always be sorry that you consecrated yourself to the doctrine of Asclepius. You've the makings of a first-rate strategist in you! What a shame! Well, I'd just as soon not have to worry about competition from you. . . . Let's go over it. The approach to the planet will be made on board one of those contraptions that can remain all but invisible if they don't get too near enemy radar. We will disembark just as the Emperor's men did on the beach of Adjemir, and our version of the Egyptian campaign will be off to a flying start! A sustained artillery assault will soon do away with these vermin. Things are going to get exciting again—we were beginning to get rusty!"

A fraternal embrace united the two comrades in arms, but the surgeon was nowhere as enthusiastic as his friend about the prospect before them.

"Look," he said. "All this is not what I'd rather do. Before rushing to arms, wouldn't it be possible to initiate negotiations with the Kveyars?"

"Ar'zog tried to at the beginning of hostilities, and his adversaries told him to go to hell!"

"That was when they thought the Fortruns were unable to offer any serious resistance. Then it was to their advantage to refuse, as the conquest of this empire, which had nobody to defend it, seemed easy enough. But now that *we're* here, the situation has changed."

"You must be joking! The ace up our sleeve is just that element of surprise. If we warn them of what we intend to do, they'll attack Dumyat immediately so that we won't have time to build up our forces. You've got a good heart, but you're not very realistic, old friend."

"Nevertheless, I'd like you to put the question to our chum Ạr'zog."

"Not on your life! I'm in complete command of this operation and I think it would be a monumental error. After all, before getting so softhearted you ought to remember that these bandits were quick enough to attack the Fortruns. I've been given the job of making it impossible for them to do any more harm, and I will unhesitatingly carry out my mission."

"As you wish," sighed Faultrier. "It's not really my affair, but I wanted you to see just what you're letting yourself in for. The die has been cast and we're about to go off to war again—only this time under conditions that are even more terrible than those on Earth."

Upon which, the surgeon went off to rejoin the gentle Katia, and to console himself with her for the savagery of men.

Early the next morning, the Commander in Chief of the Fortrun Armies passed his troops in review. He gave a solemn character to the ceremony, as he had decided to announce several promotions before they embarked for Oloch.

To the sound of the bugle, a tricolor flag surmounted with an eagle and bearing the letter F was raised as Bernard rode on horseback before the impeccably aligned formations.

He stopped first before Friancourt, his former orderly, whose duties in this sinecure had now been taken over by a robot. Drawing his saber, Bernard tapped Friancourt on the right shoulder and declared:

"*Mon brave,* you have served me long and faithfully. You didn't know how to either read or write, but the Fortruns have made another man of you, and so I now appoint you colonel of this regiment."

A robot who was standing alongside the general immediately put the braid and epaulets corresponding to his new rank on Friancourt, and Bernard moved to the next man, Queunot, who was placed in command of a company of light cavalry. The same thing happened to Bourief and Chastel, who were given command of the artillery batteries of disintegrators. Géraudont was made regimental surgeon under the command of Faultrier. Finally, Kaninski was placed in command of the Third Hussar Regiment.

This done, Bernard trotted off toward the hatchway of the *Eridanus,* the ship that was to take his troops to the site of their next battle.

One after the other the formations got underway: the first and second companies of artillery were in the lead—each with ten antigrav vehicles commanded by gunner-robots wearing superb shakos decorated with red pompons—and disappeared into the vast hold. Their numbers had been reduced to a minimum so as not to overload the ship. Next came the regiment under the orders of Friancourt, and then the units commanded by Queunot and Kaninski. Each had only fifty robots with him, a number considered sufficient to carry out this surprise attack. The last to load were the medical units, which had an anti-g ambulance equipped with an untramodern operating room.

Finally, Bernard dismounted and handed the reins of his faithful courser to his dear Tania, who like the other Russian women had been watching the ceremony. They dutifully waved their scarves in sign of farewell, but their hearts weren't in it and they had to wipe away the big tears that rolled down their cheeks.

Just as the hatch doors were about to close, the general heard a familiar voice complain:

"Somehow I've no faith in all those machines. I should have insisted on going along!"

He had barely enough time to identify the speaker. It

was the unhappy Tania, who was shaking her head sadly.

As for the Fortruns, they had not even taken the trouble to witness a spectacle so completely lacking in interest and psychedelic excitement. . . .

Chapter Six

For the second time in their lives the campaigners found themselves aboard a vessel capable of navigating through the vastness of galactic space. This time, however, they were perfectly aware of the enormous distances they were covering, and they were also extremely confident of the capacities of the perfected machine that sheltered them.

General Bernard began by debaptizing the spaceship and giving it the name *Victory of Friedland*; then he made a little speech to his colonels, all of whom were very proud of their new ranks and their splendid uniforms.

"My friends," he declared, "we are off on our first campaign. I am sure that your valor and courage will make it possible for us to win a memorable victory. The operation which we are about to undertake is in many ways similar to the Egyptian expedition. Benefiting from that experience we should be able to avoid pitfalls that might hinder our progress. The most important thing is to reach our objective without being spotted by the enemy. This time, the danger of being intercepted by the enemy fleet is minimized by the fact that our vessel can navigate subspace in temporal oscillations, so that for all practical purposes we are invisible. Besides, our adversaries are not expecting a raid from Fortrun forces because of the severe defeat they have inflicted on our friends. Finally, since the planet Oloch is quite far from the front lines, the surprise will be complete. The garrison there is probably a small one, for the population is not large. The planet's climate is difficult—the days are hot and humid. The principal sources of local wealth are the beryllium and titanium mines. I have detailed relief maps of the fort commanding this planet, and you can study them at your leisure. We intend to land some ten kilometers from the bastion we are to storm. In this way we should be able to escape detection by their radar. With the help of the robots and the anti-g vehicles, we will have to traverse a marshy zone covered with dense vegetation. According to the somewhat sketchy information furnished us by the Fortruns, who seldom left the areas in which they carried on their mining activities, there are dangerous creatures in these unhealthy marshes. It is therefore necessary that everybody stick close to the central column. When our group gets within firing range, Bourief and Chastel will lambast the fortifications with their artillery, adjusting their salvos as we advance. We will attack in two groups from opposite directions, but the second group, commanded by Friancourt, will not go over to the offensive until we have drawn the defenders to the front being attacked by Queunot's unit. Kaninski will remain in reserve and be ready to intervene wherever it becomes necessary. Any questions?"

The troopers had listened attentively to their chief's plan of attack. All of them had long experience in difficult campaigns on Earth, and the new knowledge inculcated by the oniro-suggesters made it possible for them to reason clearly and to take into account the factors added by the terrifying weapons they would now have at their command. Nevertheless, their reasoning was still in terms of comparisons with the strategy of their master: the Emperor Napoleon. Thus Chastel stood up and asked:

"General, I understand the reasoning behind this clever maneuver. After all, the Little Corporal had succeeded in fooling Nelson, and Admiral Brueys was able to disembark our expeditionary force on the beach at Figuier to the west of Alexandria. Then our divisions could mop up the Mamluks at the Pyramids. Up to this point I understand even how you intend to repeat this glorious feat of arms. But after that, I'm afraid those damned Kveyars will be able to trick us, like at Aboukir! Our attack will have alerted them, and when we want to pull out, they will pounce on us. . . ."

"An excellent observation, my old comrade! I am not unaware of this risk—especially since our fleet, unlike Brueys', is ridiculously small, this being the only ship we have! That's why it's so important that we fall upon the garrison of the Oloch fort like an eagle on its prey, giving them absolutely no chance to summon help or even to inform their headquarters of what's happening. You know as well as I do that interstellar communications are accomplished by using Hertzian waves transmitted to satellites which then relay the messages. The antennas are inside the bastion and are protected only by simple plastic domes. With the powerful artillery at your command you should have no trouble demolishing them. If by some stroke of bad luck the enemy nevertheless manages to alert the communications satellites, our *Victory of Friedland* will quickly be able to launch missiles which will put the satellites out of commission. We would then be able to pull out without any trouble."

"I see," said the gunner and nodded. "No problem then."

"And what if, against all our expectations, there should be an enemy fleet cruising in the area?" objected Queunot.

"Our teledetector will spot it at the time of our emersion and the operation will have to be postponed. But we will be operating way behind the enemy's front line, and I'd be very surprised if that happened."

"Why not use the antigravs to descend right into the fortress?" asked Kaninski.

"Simply because we would be cut to pieces by their guns before we could reach the ground. Also, there would then be no element of surprise."

"Are we to take prisoners?" asked Friancourt.

"Yes, of course! If we can get our hands on some Kveyars, Ar'zog can wring from them precious information that will help me decide on future strategy. I'm going to project some slides, so you will have no trouble identifying the Kveyars. Afterward, I'll show you a panoramic view of our objective. To begin with, here's a Kveyar without his protective spacesuit."

An extremely unattractive creature was then projected, with absolutely terrifying realism, into the center of the room. Only a little while ago the spectacle would have sown panic among the men; now that they were accustomed to all sorts of technical marvels, they merely examined the Kveyar with a critical eye.

Saffron-colored, with two long hairy arms which ended in six limp fingers, it had a huge head perched on a massive but ridiculously short neck. Three eyes, one of which was in the back of the head, and two enormous and very mobile auricular appendages, made it possible for him to become instantly aware of the approach of an enemy. Its short pawlike legs, resembling those of batrachians, made running awkward, but it could leap more than five meters where gravity conditions were similar to those on Earth.

Since the creature lived in an oxygenic atmosphere, its huge thoracic cavity boasted a pouch which contained an oxygen reserve that would last about an hour. It communicated with its own kind by telepathy; the Earthmen had been conditioned to understand them. Like all primitive creatures, the Kveyars still didn't know enough about biology to undertake a cyborgian transformation by transplanting cerebral centers into a metal robot; they therefore had to wear protective suits similar to divers' outfits when they traveled in space or on a planet with an atmosphere based on methane or ammonia.

The next slide showed the Kveyars so accoutered; the mercenaries could see pedibulator-type devices which multiplied the rather feeble musculature of the limbs by means of auxiliary motors. All in all the Kveyars' strength was inferior to that of Earthling's. Ungainly as they were, they could be easily distinguished from the massive and squat robots.

To feed themselves these creatures merely sucked nutritious liquids into mouths that were shaped like short elephant trunks. They were also able to aspirate directly the blood of animals or of their prisoners, the helmets of their protective clothing being equipped with a device that made this possible. This was something else the men had no need to ask about.

The projected image of the fort they were going to attack aroused considerably more interest. The Kveyars had the reputation of being fierce and cruel warriors who fought with determination, and the Earthmen, in spite of the new arms they had available to them, wanted to make sure that they were doing everything possible to promote their chances.

"As you can see," continued Bernard, "except for the antennas, practically nothing is visible. The radomes are camouflaged, and it's hard to distinguish them from the vegetation, whose bluish-green color is fairly close to that of the Earth. Fortunately, we have detectors that can spot underground areas and equipment that is sensitive to infrared rays, so it will be possible for us to pinpoint the fortifications. Here's an infrared shot. You can clearly see the four bastions flanking the central fortification. They all interconnect by means of underground passages. In addition, there is a mobile platform on which the flying mechanisms can set down and be transported to the underground hangars. The artillery pieces flanking them have no blind spots. Under normal circumstances these pieces are protected by shields. Some well-adjusted artillery fire should be able to jam the mobile armor and keep the pieces from forming a battery. You can see their exact emplacement in the center of each bastion. There's no possibility of reaching the fortress that way. Explosive charges could no doubt knock down the door of the main section, but then we would find ourselves in the corridors under fire from light arms, whose murderous power you are aware of. You may at this point be thinking: well, here we are at a dead end. To tell the truth, this problem had me stumped for quite a while. Then I learned from the computers of the existence of certain limited-action mechanisms that would enable us to bore tunnels rapidly. They immediately became part of my plan. If we use antigrav platforms to bring them to within a kilometer of the site, we can tunnel under the fort in less than a quarter of an hour. The tunneling equipment cannot operate at such intensity for a longer period of time, which is why we have to transport it so close to the fort itself. Our troops will attack as I have already indicated, taking advantage of the cover provided by the dense vegetation. During this time Kaninski's division will remain in reserve, eventually using the tunnels to join the assault. I am certain that the Kveyars have provided for no defense against a determined underground attack."

This time the soldiers understood their leader's ruse and manifested their approval noisily. The generous distribution of the synthetic rum and vodka that followed this talk contributed so efficaciously to the raising of morale that the men were soon all keyed up and could hardly wait for the moment in which they would give those damned Kveyars the first good hiding in their military annals.

They started brawling out the refrains of war songs, going from "Chant du Départ," to "Veillons au Salut de l'Empire." In a rush of enthusiasm, the soldiers, sensing the return of the days of victory, tried to outdo one another in shouting in their virile voices:

"Long live General Bernard! Long live the Emperor! Forward, always forward! Show them no mercy!"

The atmosphere was so charged that time now seemed to fly. Everyone was eager to make a close study of the layout of the fort's underground passages so that he would know where the command centers would be set up.

The *Victory of Friedland* worked marvelously well. The route followed by the ship avoided the ones in regular use and there were no unfortunate encounters—though on two separate occasions the teledetectors signaled unidentified ships within firing distance, and the central computer automatically turned on the mechanism that made their ship invisible. Once the alert was over, the ship returned to its normal state. Finally, when the planet Oloch was only a short distance away, the last approach maneuver was begun. It was important to come up in the shadow cone of the target underneath the surveillance satellites and far enough from the fort so that its radar could not pick up the spaceship.

This was a rather delicate exercise, even for the robot-pilot, for the least little error could be fatal—especially if the *Victory of Friedland* were to materialize too close to the ground.

As it happened, the ship appeared out of nowhere at a thousand meters from the surface of the ocean and immediately descended to sea level. Everything had gone off smoothly, and the radio receivers picked up no signal that could be interpreted as meaning that the ship had been spotted. The advance toward the fort continued at a reduced speed. Soon the continent was within sight, and the flight continued just above the treetops, following the terrain but avoiding inhabited areas.

Finally, after an additional fifteen minutes of flight—during which the soldiers gave their equipment a last check—the telescopic supports of the vessel gently settled down in a clearing.

The importance of the antigravs immediately became clear, since the shock absorbers of the ship's landing disks sank two meters into the marshy soil. Overhead flew swarms of enormous insects whose usual activities had been upset by the unexpected landing of this huge craft.

Before opening the hatches and launching his troops, Bernard gave them some final advice:

"Soldiers! We have lived through some terrible moments together. Our transfer into a universe formerly unknown to us offers a unique opportunity to demonstrate the valor of the campaigners of the Grand Army. The hour of combat has come: see to it that you give a good account of yourself; remember that from the summit of the firmament, eternity looks down upon you! The peoples of the galaxy are going to learn that henceforth they will have to deal with Earthlings. Remember the verse that goes:

'Upon the safety of our nation

Depends that of the universe;
If ever we are conquered
The world will go in chains. . . .'

"These words take on new dimensions, because if the Kveyars continue to sweep all before them, the Earth itself will soon be their prey."

Reasonably content with the formulas he had employed—even if they did paraphrase certain exhortations of the Emperor during the Egyptian campaign—the general took his place in a landing vehicle, unsheathed his saber, and gave the order for his battalions to disembark from the ship.

One after another, the landing vehicles started north. Relaxing in their comfortable seats and protected by the transparent domes of the cabins, the new colonels gaily hummed martial refrains, the following being a particular favorite.

"Do you know why I'm fond of you?
Do you know why, my trusty old equipment?
It's because you've been my best friend
Ever since I joined the regiment."

Soon, however, they were aware of the first of several potential difficulties. A few meters beneath the vehicles, the glaucous surface of the swamp was heaving in an unsettling manner. The bluish mold and mildew that covered its unhealthy waters would sometimes part to disclose repugnant shapes—some smooth, others alive with tentacles. Each was more fantastic than the others.

The thick fog easily pierced by the infrared noctoscopes hid a multitude of vaporous creatures. Disquieting phantoms uncoiled, dilacerated, and were reborn a little farther away under other forms: hideous caricatures worthy of the most horrible nightmares.

"Say," Chastel grumbled over the communications system, "do you see those shapes that seem to be laughing at us? I've a good mind to take a shot at them, just to see. . . ."

73

"Don't try anything stupid!" Bernard thundered in a commanding voice. "We don't want to be spotted. Nobody is to use his weapons unless he's attacked. Besides, we are quite safe here in the cabins, and I don't think these hobgoblins are dangerous. You would do better to keep an eye on the surface of the swamp."

"I agree with you," Bourief chimed in approvingly. "I've just seen something striking out at my vehicle. It must have been at least ten meters long. . . ."

During the next ten minutes or so, they moved forward without incident. In ranks of four the hovercars planed over the marshy surface. Then suddenly, without warning, the monsters began to attack. Five vehicles driven by robots were seized by the tentacles of horrible creatures that looked like enormous octopuses. Before the pilots could react, their machines wobbled and struck the water. The maws of the monsters immediately closed over the hulls and dragged them down into the depths.

For a few seconds the mechanical defenses elaborated by the Fortruns continued the combat. Bolts of light illuminated the muddy liquid. Bits of spongy flesh surfaced, and enormous bubbles rose and burst. Shreds of plastic floated about for a moment, but the wriggling of the tentacles at the point of impact and the waves stirred up by the hopeless fight of the robots soon ceased, and once more calm returned to the bog.

"Blood and thunder!" swore Bernard. "Things are beginning badly. Let's get a little altitude. Perhaps we'll be all right if we climb to twenty meters. It's a lucky thing that none of us was dragged down by these monsters. Watch it, now—this spot doesn't look too healthy. They must have jaws stronger than steel to be able to cut through the metal the way they did."

The column continued along its way. In the distance a slight glow showed that dawn was near. The *Victory of Friedland* had long since disappeared behind them, and the troopers could henceforth count only on themselves.

A new subject for anxiety soon arose. The fog around the hovercars became luminescent, and a curious crackling sound came over the communications apparatus. The detectors, however, did not indicate any special problem: to all appearances the way ahead was clear. And yet the vehicles were being subjected to an inexplicable braking force, and it became necessary to keep increasing power to maintain speed.

The warning signals of the miniaturized control center soon explained what was happening. The energy of the vehicles was being absorbed—sucked in, as it were—by the phosphorescent clouds whose brilliance continued to increase.

In a short time the red blinker which was supposed to give the alarm if there was a loss of motor power began to flutter on all the control boards. Even the automatic pilots were being drained by this phenomenon, and their reactions became slow and imprecise. If things went on like that, the entire expedition would soon plunge into the swamp, where the monstrous creatures awaited them.

Bernard therefore decided to take decisive action, and he ordered:

"Disconnect the guidance system, take over manual control, and see if you can't climb above all this filth!"

The robots and the soldiers immediately obeyed. Things improved. Little by little the machines regained altitude and the seepage of energy was diminished. The voracious gas was not, however, so easily discouraged. Enormous bubbles that looked like blisters kept breaking on the surface of the swamp. Greenish nebulosities then began pursuing the vehicles, stretching long diaphanous fingers toward them, as though to latch on to their escaping prey.

On several occasions, strange visions appeared on the viewing screens: Earth landscapes that had been more or less forgotten; the smiling faces of women. But the soldiers did not let themselves be tempted by these phantasms; the edge of the forest could be seen on the horizon, and the blush of the rising sun contributed to dissipating the unhealthy mists.

Bernard was then faced with a new problem. Ought he to fly over the thick wood, staying just above the treetops—and thus risking discovery by the Kveyar garrison—or ought he to profit from the thick fronds to proceed under cover?

The attacks they had undergone over the marsh contributed to the choice of the first solution. Besides, the interweaving of the vines and branches would have made an advance at ground level very difficult.

For a little while the general found no reason not to congratulate himself on his decision. The vehicles, flying close to the tops of the trees, were in no way bothered. The camouflage mechanisms and the absorption of detection waves had been set in motion, and it would have taken an extremely attentive observer to spot the vehicles noiselessly gliding through the quiet air.

Nevertheless, the creatures who lived in the forest didn't allow themselves to be made light of so easily. Immense winged things nesting in the thick foliage came out of their hiding places and, from a prudent distance, escorted the intruders who had dared invade their domain. Little by little they gathered into two groups, continually swelled by new arrivals. Their number so increased that Bernard, uneasy, decided to take temporary advantage of the cover of the trees, since such a swarm of predators was likely to draw the attention of enemy lookouts.

One after another the hovercars descended into the luxuriant forest, remaining immobile under the cover of thick branches. The soldiers profited from these few moments of respite to inspect the surrounding vegetation and could not keep from admiring the spectacle before them.

In the blue light sifting through the large leaves they could see innumerable corollas of sumptuously colored flowers. Similar to epiphytic orchids, they grew in bunches on the trunks and branches and offered their calices, filled with honeylike liquids, to the clouds of diaphanous-winged insects that came to plunder them. They were of the most subtle shades, and they created a veritable symphony of color which enchanted the staring men.

But Bernard remained indifferent to this spectacle:

he had good reason to, since, far from dispersing, the winged creatures were now hovering above the expedition in a compact group. They had to be got rid of at any cost. The general had a variety of means at his disposal, and he decided on the one that seemed most discreet: toxic gases. On his orders, all the landing vehicles began to fire, sending into the heart of the hovering group tiny plastic spheres containing a compressed product that volatilized as soon as the capsule opened.

In a few moments, the worrisome creatures were dispersed. A good hundred or so of the birds were struck down by the poison and spiraled to the ground; the others didn't wait around to find out what had happened, and took to their wings without delay.

Satisfied, Bernard was about to have his columns start up again when flexible and elastic thongs covered with suction cups fell on the vehicles and on the corpses of the birds; the general had unwarily attracted carnivorous vines, which now attacked as if they had been given some signal. Trapped in these elastic bonds, the vehicles were unable to fight free even by using their full power. For a moment, Bernard thought that his epic adventure was going to end ignominiously in this forest inhabited by demonic creatures.

But the computers on board were able to analyze the situation faster than a human brain could, and they found a spectacular solution: all the de-icers on the vehicles went into immediate action and brought the fuselages to an elevated temperature.

Atrociously burned, the carnivorous plants soon gave up; they released their prey, and the liberated hovercars shot above the treetops like so many cannon balls.

Unfortunately, a few of them struck against enormous branches; six vehicles were completely destroyed and fifteen variously damaged. Among them were those belonging to Bourief and Friancourt. Immediately rescued by those around them, they abandoned ship and climbed helter-skelter aboard another hovercar.

Twelve vehicles proved too damaged to continue and

were left behind; Bernard had also lost twenty-four robots.

It was a heavy blow to an expeditionary corps that
had not yet gone into battle. . . .

Chapter Seven

Somewhat dispirited, Bernard decided to ask Faultrier what he thought of the situation. The doctor had just placed Bourief in a tissue regenerator, since during the accident to his hovercar the gunner had received a head wound. A sly smile on his lips, the doctor listened to his leader's woes.

"The situation is none too good," noted the general. "I wonder if I underestimated the natural defense capacities of this damned planet. The Fortruns never said a word about any of these creatures. Those people certainly don't seem to be all that interested in their territorial possessions, and I'm beginning to wonder if we weren't the first to have ever set foot in that cursed jungle."

"Bah!" replied his friend. "You didn't really think you could carry out your mission without a hitch, did you? The vastness of this new world contains many unknown factors. It's only normal that the flora and fauna of these planets be different from those back on our good old Earth. With the perfected weapons and machines that you've got working for you, there's really not much to fear from whatever creatures inhabit Oloch. Even with the losses you've sustained, your forces are still more than sufficient to attack the fort. Besides, none of us has been badly hurt, and that's the important thing!"

"You're right. I'm not going to let myself be depressed by a few minor incidents! After all, I should have realized that an extraterrestrial planet would be more dangerous than the plains of the Po or the Russian steppes. . . . How is Bourief doing?"

"Extremely well. With the wonderful equipment I

have, wounds are healed in a few minutes. The Fortruns even gave me a complete set of spare limbs. Do you remember when they took a few patches of cutaneous tissue from each of us? Well, thanks to some chromosomic cellular equipment, the computers have been able to assure the *in vitro* development of tissue cultures and supply me with an organ bank. My robot surgeons are infinitely more skillful than I am, and they are capable of replacing any missing part of our organism. Isn't that amazing?"

"Fantastic! But I'm afraid that most of your scientific explanations are over my head, you know. Unlike you, I had no very advanced biological training, and this all still seems very Utopian to me! When I think of the men I served with who now have only one arm or who have to hop around on one leg . . . when I remember the suffering on the battlefields . . . If only all this knowledge could be made available to those on Earth!"

"I'm the first to be sorry that it cannot. I even feel a little ashamed of having so much power. I wonder if one day it will be possible to teach these wonders to our compatriots."

"Don't count on it! You know that the Fortruns absolutely refuse to intervene in the affairs of developing planets. It's one of their basic laws. We were brought here to fight for them, and that's the only thing we have a right to do. I have no illusions about what will happen. If I manage to liquidate the Kveyars, I'm reasonably sure that Ar'zog will arrange things so that I'm in no position to cause trouble. However, I have no intention of letting myself be taken advantage of. But enough of that—there's no point in rattling on like this about problems that are still in the future. We have to begin at the beginning, and that means we have to take this fort."

The general signed off then and gave the orders for his troops to move on again. This time he chose to proceed under the cover of the branches and to keep the outside temperature of the vehicles' hulls very high. The energy outlay would be considerable, but there were only another ten kilometers or so to go, and the important thing was not to be spotted.

During the rest of the trip there were a number of new incidents: carnivorous plants tried to attack the hovercars; enormous serpents wrapped around the upper branches attempted to crush some of the vehicles in their powerful coils; the luminescent fog still interfered with radio communications; but on the whole all these assaults were repulsed without loss, and the vehicles, tacking about through the giant stands of trees that surrounded them, came within the vicinity of their goal by the end of the morning.

Following the sacrosanct principles of all armies, Bernard began by seeing to it that his troops were fed: men cannot be sent into battle on an empty stomach. Then he advanced his hovercar to the edge of the forest and carefully examined the fortifications with a telescope. As expected, there was little to see besides the radomes. A few robots were milling around a vehicle that seemed very like their own hovercars. Two of them climbed on board, and the craft flew off in a direction opposite the position of the attackers. The mercenaries apparently had not been spotted. Satisfied, the general quit his observation post and signaled his colonels to gather around him. When they had done so, he gave them their final instructions.

"I'm counting on you to obey my orders down to the smallest detail," he declared. "Nobody is to go off half-cocked or take unnecessary risks. The robots are there to do the fighting, and all you have to do is issue orders to them. Don't forget that the weapons the Kveyars have are a hundred times more deadly than those we are used to. Because of this, the battalion leaders are to place their command vehicles far behind the front lines. Also remember that your mission is a diversionary one and that there are to be no impulsive assaults. The fortress is to be taken from below. As soon as Bourief and Chastel have set up their artillery, they will open fire. I will then begin the tunneling operations. Let's hope that you'll be keeping the Kveyars too busy for them to have time to detect my tunnelers. One last

81

thing: keep the radomes in your sights, and at the least sign that there has been a radio emission, have your ship demolish the satellites. That's all. Good luck!"

More keyed up than he wanted the others to know, Bernard went off to join the robot-diggers and take up his position in one of the tunnelers. For him, everything depended on what happened during the next hour. If he should be victorious, the Fortruns would turn over large forces to him; if he should be defeated, he was sure they would dismiss him from his command. Should that happen, the ambitions of General Bernard would be forever unrealizable.

The sudden rumble of the missiles and the hiss of the disintegrators made him jump. The discovery operation had begun.

As soon as the cloud of smoke had cleared somewhat, Bernard could see that the radomes had disappeared. Satisfied with the skill of his gunners, he ordered his contingent to start the tunnelers going.

This experience was something entirely new for the Earthling. The machines moved ahead smoothly, tossing the loose earth and the pulverized rock behind them. As they advanced, they played out cables so they could maintain contact with the surface. In this way, Bernard was able to assure himself that his directions were being followed scrupulously: the fort was being submitted to a sustained pounding, and the Kveyars, surprised, were doing absolutely nothing. A few guns tried to form a battery with which to return fire, but embrasure shots silenced them, and for a long time the projectiles of the attackers were the only ones to plow up the soil.

But this situation did not last long, for some Kveyar robots managed to slip out of the fort through secret doors situated some distance away, and they soon began to return fire. Five or six armored vehicles joined their position.

Queunot's troops immediately went into counter-offensive action and rapidly liquidated the group. Nevertheless, once they had got over the first moment of surprise, the enemy came to grips with the situation and new robots kept appearing from well-hidden tunnels.

The regiments of the Fortrun army, carefully camouflaged by the dense foliage, had no difficulty in containing them. The Kveyars had scarcely surfaced before they found themselves in an inferno, with bullets and atomic grenades raining down on them. The only way they could even try to escape was by flattening themselves on the ground.

All in all, the attackers had the situation well in hand.

Satisfied, Bernard turned his attention to his own units. Kaninski's company was following behind him in good order, and according to the calculations of their computers, the tunnelers were almost directly under the fortress.

The cavity detectors provided a fairly clear view of the network of underground passageways the Kveyars had dug in the depths of the rock. In the center, in an armored casing, was the energy pile that fed the fort. It was a place to avoid, since the problems of radioactive pollution could be severe. All around this area, the control installations and the various kinds of equipment needed to operate the fort formed two symmetrical tori. On an upper level were the living quarters and the munitions bunkers, linked to the heavy guns by vertical shafts.

The first objective of the attackers was on the lowest level, where there were hangars containing supplies and anti-g mechanisms, as well as a few tunnelers.

There was no sign of any preparations to repel an underground assault. All the robots were hastening toward the passages leading to the surface.

The networks were mostly in spiral form, the corridors sloping gently from one level to another.

Guided by its computer, the lead tunneler made a sharp upward turn that brought it to a ninety-degree angle from its original path. In only a few seconds Bernard's advance sections would debouch in the very heart of the enemy fortress.

"Ready, Kaninski?" asked the general.

"Ready, sir! We'll fall on them and it will be all over before they know what hit them!"

"That's right! Watch out, though. See to it that your robots are accurately programmed, as I'd like to take a few prisoners."

"All right."

Before they came to the first underground passageway, the lead vehicles spread out in a fan formation, and ten of them emerged simultaneously. A few surprised robots were liquidated before they could give the alarm. One after another the tunneling machines reached their objective and disgorged their troops.

The Fortrun robots immediately swarmed forth, surprising those few defenders who tried to block their advance. With only minor losses they reached the vertical shafts and, using their anti-gs, quickly attained the upper levels.

Bernard followed their advance on a screen in his command post, pointing out zones of resistance and dispatching troops to the trouble spots. Kaninski fought alongside his own regiment.

The Kveyars soon enough realized what was happening and lowered bulkheads to seal off the underground passageways. Unhappily for them, Bernard's troops were accompanied by a few drilling machines, and these obstacles were quickly demolished. Kveyar reinforcements called to the rescue were unable to prevent the rampaging Fortrun robots from reaching the central power station and seizing the controls before the defenders could blow them up. All the gates of the surface defense posts were opened. Immediately, the general gave the attack signal to the regiments of Friancourt and Queunot, who swept before them the few enemy units still putting up resistance and in their turn invaded the fortress, this time from above. The shako-adorned robots accomplished wonders.

Bereft of instructions from the central command post, the Kveyars, left to their own initiative, put up only sporadic resistance. After having tried to slow the advance of the invaders by setting off explosive charges at various intersections, only a few determined Kveyar robots had withdrawn into isolated sectors to continue the fight. A junction was soon established between the Fortrun forces attacking from above and Bernard's troops coming up from below.

The struggle was over. It had all gone smoothly enough, and at this point the general left his command post and began to inspect the area.

Protected by an escort of vigilant robots ready to fire in case of danger, he reached the Kveyar command post, where he found Queunot and Friancourt waiting.

"Congratulations, gentlemen," exclaimed Bernard as soon as he saw them. And then once more echoing Napoleon he announced: *"Soldats, je suis content de vous!* Our adversaries were completely taken by surprise. As we foresaw, they concentrated all their forces on your units. All I had to do was occupy the underground passages, and the resistance was laughable. The fort is ours. I don't intend to linger here, but before leaving I'd like to look over our booty."

"General," announced Queunot with a satisfied air, "I've some good news for you. We were able to take four prisoners. Before they had a chance to flee, they were paralyzed on the spot by these wonderful Fortrun gadgets."

"Excellent, excellent! You've really distinguished yourself—but then I expected no less of you."

Going up to him, Bernard took his Legion of Honor from his own tunic and pinned it on Queunot's breast, saying:

"You will be the first to be personally decorated by me. Continue to serve me faithfully and you will not regret it. I have great plans for the future and I will not forget my old friends. Bring in the captives!"

Settling comfortably into one of the chairs, he took from his pocket a plug of synthetic tobacco, and began chewing away in evident pleasure.

While the robots were getting the prisoners, the general examined the room in which he found himself. It resembled in a way the command posts of the spaceships; there were keyboards for consulting the computers and transmitting orders, and there were also viewing

Pierre Barbet

screens and control panels and which flickered a multitude of lights.

Evidently Kveyar technology was very similar to that
of the Fortruns. They made war with the help of
computers which had been fed information on the military situation, and then they acted on instructions based
on the probability for success of any given action. Apparently an attack on Oloch had been judged highly improbable, which was why it had gone off so well. This
was just what Bernard had expected, and he rubbed his
hands together in satisfaction.

But his reflections on the matter went no further, for
just then the robots came in with the prisoners.

The Kveyars resembled perfectly the images shown
him by the Fortruns; these creatures seemed considerably more courageous and determined than the allies of
the Earthmen. In spite of the immobility caused by the
paralyzers, their eyes darted defiance at the victors.
However, Bernard thought he could also discern in
these glances a glimmer of admiration and amazement,
for they certainly were not expecting to find themselves
in the presence of creatures unknown to them.

His inspection over, the general tried to put his intelligence in commmunication with theirs so that he could
proceed to a formal interrogation. To his great surprise,
he came up against a barrier that prevented him from
carrying on the kind of telepathic communication he
had been taught by the Fortruns.

"What's this?" he grumbled. "What's happening?"

"It's absolutely impossible to read their minds," confirmed Queunot.

"But we've been conditioned to be able to do so!
These horrors must have powers we weren't warned
about. . . ."

"I'm surprised the Fortruns weren't aware of these
astonishing powers," noted Friancourt. "I've got a
feeling these creatures know exactly what we're thinking. Suppose we try using a little primitive persuasion
to untie their tongues?"

"In other words, you want to put them to the question by using torture?"

"Exactly!"

"Well, that's a possibility," approved Bernard as he stroked his chin. "After all, we are at war."

"What do you say to tickling the soles of their feet with a torch?"

"Interesting, but a little crude. We know nothing about their anatomy or their nervous system. I don't want to run the risk of killing them. No, we have something better than those primitive techniques. Bring me some neuro-tetanizers. I seem to remember that they've been adjusted to act on the different races in this galactic sector."

A robot went off to get requested instruments from one of the tunneling machines. While waiting, Bernard stood up and approached one of the captives.

Except for his protective clothing, the Kveyar seemed to have no special equipment, but the Earthlings did not know enough about the technical achievements of his enemies to be sure of this. In any case, the Kveyar and his companions had extremely efficient protection against psychic probing.

Though their motor impulses were blocked, their nerve centers and intellectual responses were completely intact; this made a few experiments feasible.

At this point the robot returned with the neuro-tetanizing whip.

"Listen carefully!" warned Bernard, taking up the instrument. "You probably know very well how this gadget works. It is going to lash your nerve endings and cause extreme pain. By temporarily liberating your muscles, it will bring on unpleasant contractions. Would you care to think things over?"

Receiving no response, he set the instrument for maximum effect, attached the two electrodes to the neck of one of the prisoners, and discharged a series of shocks.

The results were totally negative. For the next five minutes the general stubbornly kept at his victim, but it was useless.

"It's one of two things. Either he's been trained to resist torture or else he's equipped with a neutralizer. In either case I'm wasting my time, and we'll have to try something else. . . ."

The officer thought for a few moments and then sent a new message to the prisoners.

"I haven't much time, so this is my final warning. If you don't lower your psychic barrier, you are going to regret not having been more cooperative. I have some personal techniques that will work much better than this highly perfected whip. . . ."

The creatures didn't flinch; no psychic signal reached the Earthling.

"Fine! Remember that you've brought it upon yourselves," spat Bernard, who unsheathed his saber and began to slice through the protective clothing of one of the captives. With his left hand he brutally ripped away the clothing beneath the outer garment and bared the viscous and rounded belly of the Kveyar.

Smiling sadistically, he slowly promenaded the razor-sharp saber, making parallel zebra stripes on the skin. A greenish chyle began to ooze from the wounds, but the prisoner remained silent.

With the point of his blade the general lifted a flap of skin, and seizing it between his fingers, pulled sharply, tearing off a strip some ten centimeters long. He repeated this procedure five times.

A few drops of opalescent liquid began to well up on the forehead of his victim and roll down the hideous face, but still the Kveyar never so much as flinched.

Changing his tactics, the torturer then placed his saber on the cornea of the right eye and shot out the warning thought:

"Make up your mind or I'll gouge it out . . . !"

At that point he received a terrified message:

"You can't really be thinking of doing that! Nobody could be so cruel! The demon of evil must be within you."

A satisfied smile played over Bernard's lips.

"Obviously," he noted, "the good old methods are the best! If necessary, I'm prepared to rip out all three of your eyes and cut you into bits. Answer me! How do you manage to place this barrier over your mind?"

"Take that thing away and I'll tell you everything!

There's a very fine net of minute fillets under the skin of my cranium. We have several of them here and they are easy to install. A robot can supply you with one if you wish."

"Show me a few of them."

One of the captive soldiers immediately went to a vast closet in the room and took out several boxes which he gave to Bernard.

On opening these, the general found they contained gossamerlike webs carefully sealed in transparent plastic bags. A tape reel which undoubtedly contained instructions for their installation accompanied the webs.

"Fine! Now tell me why we were able to beat you so easily?"

"The reason is obvious. We make war with the aid of computers that are continually being fed information on the forces we face, their position, power, and state of mind. The probability of an attack on Oloch was minimal and therefore the garrison was very small. In addition, we had not been placed on the alert. All resistance was therefore bound to fail."

"Good. And now I would like to know what your present plans are."

The Kveyar hesitated a moment, but the sight of the point of the still menacing saber seemed to decide him to continue his confidences.

"Until now we were in no particular hurry. Time was on our side, as the Fortruns are hedonists incapable of adequately defending themselves. By occupying their planets and factories one by one, we were removing from them the possibility of fighting off our fleet. Dumyat would have fallen into our hands almost without a struggle. Our squadrons are therefore dispersed, slowly encircling the enemy capital. It seems, alas, that those abject and frightened creatures have found unknown allies of a terrifying savagery. This alters the situation considerably."

"To be sure. But since not one of you managed to escape from Oloch, your computers are unaware of the new situation. The destruction of the fortress will remain inexplicable. That will be strange and will pose an

Pierre Barbet

enigma to your computers, but as they know nothing about us, I would be astonished if they were to find out how to ward off my plans."

Horror made the prisoner fall silent a few seconds, and then he asked:

"Are you going to leave us here to perish with this bastion?"

"Exactly! I have no further need of you, and the Fortruns are incapable of guarding prisoners correctly!"

"Spare me!" begged the captive. "I swear to serve you faithfully and to advise you. I am a specialist on military questions and you can get precious information from me that will help your vessels in their fight against ours."

"Changed your tune, have you?" grumbled Bernard. "Nobody had done you the least bit of harm and yet you had no pity on the Fortruns!"

"I beg you, spare my life. . . ."

"Pity!" chorused the other captives.

"All right. I will let myself be persuaded. You will remain on board my vessel. After all, I may still have need of you. But careful, now. The least attempt to escape, the least bit of false information, and I will run my saber through you."

Beaten, the Kveyars let their heads droop sadly. Never in their most horrible nightmares had they envisaged so terrible a situation: to be the captives of primitive brutes of unbelievable savagery.

"Take them away!" ordered the general. "Just leave this one and have him show you their archives and secret material, which you can then load on board our ships. Be quick about it. I want to be out of here in half an hour. You are to place an atomic bomb in the nuclear power center and set it to go off in an hour."

Bernard turned his back on the prisoners and, followed by Queunot, went to the nearest of the anti-g shafts. Kaninski remained behind to carry out his leader's orders.

The Earthlings were jubilant. The whole operation had gone off without a hitch, and the old soldiers were confident of the future.

Chapter Eight

An apocalyptic spectacle was provided by conditions on the surface. The area of the fort was sown with innumerable craters, and despite the use of "clean" bombs, the spacesuits had to be set for maximum protection against radiation.

A few robots were guarding the ruins. The edge of the forest had been completely dug up by the defenders' projectiles, and a tangle of vegetal debris extended as far as the eye could see.

A hovercar picked up the general to take him to the *Victory of Friedland*. Just before it took off, Bourief came to report.

"Congratulations!" exclaimed Bernard. "Your firing was remarkably accurate, and you followed my orders to the letter. Keep it up. I'm awarding you a gunner's medal."

The artilleryman bowed in sign of thanks, but he remained sad and stiff.

"All right, what's the matter? You seem out of spirits. Were you hoping for the cross? Well, perhaps some other time. . . ."

"No, General, I'm very pleased with the honor you've bestowed on me, but I'm afraid I won't be able to celebrate this one. I have bad news for you. Chastel is dead."

"What! *Sacrénom!* How did it happen?"

"It was fate, I guess. One of the last shots fired by the Kveyars landed right in the middle of his command post. We didn't find so much as a trace of him."

"The vermin! They'll pay for this! That's the first man we've lost, and our forces are thin enough. . . . I would like to have had many more officers as brave and

92

devoted as he was! Well, it can't be helped. War is war."

"Alas, yes. We've lost a good comrade, one I will never forget. He was always cheerful and ready to help anybody who needed it."

"Until further notice, you're to take over command of the artillery. Have them sound assembly. We're leaving in half an hour and everybody's to be on board. After we're out of here, the fort is going to blow up."

Bourief saluted and left the vehicle to carry out the orders he had received. Bernard's hovercar took off immediately and flew directly to the spaceship that was waiting at the rendezvous area.

All the regiments joined him there within the half-hour deadline. A quick roll call showed that the losses had been very light: no more than twenty robots.

Except for the death of Chastel, the operation had gone off as smoothly as possible, which boded well for the future. The campaigners, habituated by long years of combat to seeing their comrades disappear, took the news without outward signs of exaggerated distress. Most of them knew they would probably not live long, but the acceptance of that hard truth made for the grandeur of armies. It was best not to think about it too much.

The *Victory of Friedland* embarked all the regiments without any further incident. This time there was no need for the returning vehicles to traverse the jungle, and the few giant birds that ventured too close were killed before they could attack. The spaceship took off, launching as it went a few missiles aimed at the remaining artificial satellites. The ship's tele-radars showed that there were no enemy squadrons in the area, and the *Victory of Friedland* calmly penetrated subspace and began the voyage back.

During the trip, Bernard kept to his cabin, meditating on his plans for the future. There was no doubt the Fortruns were going to put him in command of powerful squadrons. It was up to him to know how to profit from this. He would see to it that his protectors got what they wanted; he would fight the Kveyars to the bitter end. It shouldn't be too difficult to beat them by taking them by surprise. Since they used computers to decide on tactics, all he had to do to outwit them, was to attack in the very places where their computers indicated that an attack was most improbable. And since the Fortruns had similar computers, he need only consult them to determine the points at which enemy resistance would be strong.

Afterward, when the vast Fortrun domains were in his hands, what could be easier than to simply confiscate all their squadrons? As the master of space, he, Bernard, would become the emperor of the galaxy. Napoleon himself could not boast such a destiny!

To carry out his ambitious projects, he would have to use the greatest discretion. As it happened, the Kveyars had just furnished him with miraculous means by which he could dissimulate his thoughts. The general therefore sent for his prisoners, and under Friancourt's watchful eye he had them insert the marvelous net of integrated supercircuits fixed on thin films of flexible plastic.

Once this had been done, he felt much easier about things, but his constantly alert Machiavellian mind suggested a further scheme, one that would totally protect him from the results of any indiscretions. One evening, he ordered the robots on duty to diffuse a toxic gas into the cell in which his prisoners were kept, and once the Kveyars were lifeless, he had the five robots stage a mock struggle with disintegrators and fire on the inert bodies.

The simulated combat caused a great uproar and confirmed Bernard's story that the captives had tried to escape and take over the ship. Their bodies were unceremoniously pushed out into space. As for the robots who had taken part in the "fight," their memories were modified so as to conform to the report given by the general.

Everything was now as it should be. Two days later the *Victory of Friedland* landed at the Dumyat astroport. An account of the exciting events of the expedition had been radioed ahead, and this time several

Fortruns accompanied Ar'zog to welcome the victorious soldiers.

Even more astonishing was the hearty fanfare that made the air resound with its old-fashioned blare. This was how the Russian women had chosen to demonstrate that they had not forgotten their lovers.

With the colonels up front, the regiments that had participated in this hardy surprise attack paraded in perfect order before their leader, who was seated on his faithful stallion which was prancing with joy.

The ceremony once over, the robots went off to their quarters to be readjusted. Disconnected, they would await the next expedition.

The Earthlings turned toward the astroport buildings. News of the victory had vaguely tempted the Fortruns from their lethargic pleasures and about ten of them were waiting for the men.

The general took advantage of the occasion to make his report to Ar'zog, who warmly congratulated him. Bernard began the tale of his exploits, emphasizing the fact that it would be necessary to abandon the tactic of depending on the computers and institute one in which the enemy would be attacked at the least likely spot. The general soon noticed, however, that Ar'zog was listening only distractedly: the robots had brought in the booty captured in the fort, and all the Fortruns had rushed to rummage through it like children, eagerly searching for some exotic object that might provide some new pleasure for their blasé senses. They were completely uninterested in the secret archives, which must nevertheless have contained some interesting information.

Soon, however, they found what they were looking for in the form of a crystal mounted in a complicated apparatus. This gem modulated sounds and lights, projecting from itself splendidly colored forms to the music of a subtle and engaging symphony.

Ar'zog, of course, was by no means indifferent to this new toy, and wanted an opportunity to enjoy it. But Bernard lost his temper.

"How can anyone be so idiotic?" he stormed. "It's

not surprising that your enemies are busy seizing control of the empire! All you can think of is amusing yourself and enjoying life. I've just risked my own neck—and my companions'—in an attempt to pull you out of this mess. One of my dearest comrades, Chastel, died during the attack, and all you can think of is to search for new amusements! I realize that our lives are not terribly important to you, but I have only an extremely limited headquarters group at my command as it is, and if I lose a colonel every time we go into action, it will be difficult to direct your squadrons. I have absolutely no confidence in your robots, who completely lack any initiative!"

"Come now, my friend, don't get angry," Ar'zog said in a mollifying tone. "Long years of civilization have left us blasé, and anything new is very much in demand. I must congratulate you on having thought to bring us this apparatus. But let's get back to your problems. I understand how you feel, and in spite of your reproaches I have already given thought to the manpower problem. You are extremely precious to us and would be difficult to replace, which is why we took our precautions before you left. Just look behind you."

The general turned around and almost swallowed his plug of tobacco; coming toward him was a flesh-and-blood, smiling Chastel, who came to a halt and smartly saluted.

Stupefied, Bernard seized Chastel's arm, gropingly felt the flesh, and even placed his hand on the robust chest so that he could feel the regular heartbeats.

"It's black magic!" he mumbled. "How can it be possible? The body of my unfortunate companion was blown to pieces by Kveyar artillery."

"Come, now," the Fortrun said reproachfully. "You must forget all your superstitions. After all, we did reeducate you! Your doctors have spare limbs among their medical gear, so why shouldn't we be able to recreate a whole human body? Each of your cells has chromosomes that contain all the information necessary to make a twin of you! Our biological synthesizers have had the time to work on this since your arrival here."

"In other words, this is a brother of Chastel, whom he resembles in every way?"

"Exactly. With only one minor difference: his brain contains only the information from the past that was present in the Earthling's brain before he left for Oloch. Actually, our computers probe your brains every night in order to register the events you have lived through during the day."

Bernard noted this fact privately and congratulated himself on having kept the secret of the protective nets.

"In this way," continued Ar'zog, "we have at every moment a reserve of Earthlings who can take over in case of accident."

"Do you mean that I, too, have a twin brother?" asked the general in astonishment.

"Of course! With the kind of fragile bodies you have, you are all living on borrowed time. We have to take our precautions."

"Unbelievable! How is it that I've never run across my 'brother'?"

"Our archives keep your replacements in hibernation, except during the periods when their memories are being fed. Once this is done, they are put back to sleep. . . . But now I have to leave you. I can hardly wait to take advantage of this marvelous crystal. We'll have copies made and distributed to everyone. If you'd like one, all you have to do is ask."

Bernard was too astonished to think of detaining the Fortrun any longer, and Ar'zog profited from his confusion to slip away.

The Earthling, though now accustomed to the wonders of Fortrun technology, decided to check for himself, and he asked a few questions of the new Chastel that would enable him to test just how closely the copy conformed to the original.

"At ease," he ordered Chastel. "Well! I'm delighted that a good companion has been saved for me. Nevertheless, I would like to ask you a few questions. Where were you born?"

The artilleryman seemed surprised by this question.

97

"In Colmar, General. You know very well. I'm an Alsatian. . . ."

"Hmph! Just answer my questions and skip the commentary, please. I simply want to assure myself that you are in complete possession of all your faculties. What was the name of your general during the Russian campaign?"

"Weelwartz."

"What army corps did you belong to?"

"The Third, under the command of Elchingen."

"Fine. Now since you're an artillery man, tell me how many guns you had in your battery."

"Four, of course."

"Who commanded the first brigade of the Third Corps?"

"Mouriez. That formation included the Sixth Light Cavalry, the Eleventh Hussars, the Fourth Infantry, the Twenty-eighth Infantry, and some Wurtemberg troops."

"Marvelous," said the general. "I can see that you've forgotten nothing. One last question. What were the arms and uniform of the Polish hussars?"

"A 1796-type musket, a Year-IV saber, a black shako with white braid and black plume. The uniform was a blue pelisse, scarlet dolman, yellow buttons."

"Well done! I can't get over it. You are to retain your command. And now, rejoin your comrades and don't be surprised at their reaction. During the fight on Oloch your older brother was killed and they don't expect to see you. Explain to them that we all have doubles who can replace us in case of accident."

"At your orders, General!"

Bernard remained sunk in thought for a moment. Obviously his allies had supernatural powers. He hoped that they knew nothing about the psycho-protective nets, or he would soon be unmasked!

Just then Tania shot out of nowhere like a cannon ball, and throwing her arms around Bernard's neck, she gave him the kind of kiss that leaves a man breathless. Then she launched into a dithyramb praising the courage, valor, and wisdom of her lord and master before going on to say in no uncertain terms what she thought of this business of the doubles created by the Fortruns.

"Myself," she declared unequivocally, "I'm suspicious of these people! A girl can't be sure of anything anymore. A funny kind of business that is! In any case, I warn you not to 'accidentally' crawl into the bed of one of my doubles. I'd never forgive you! If necessary, I'll have my hair dyed green so that you'll have no excuse for making a mistake!"

"You needn't worry! You and I have been through too much together for me to ever cheat on you," the general reassured her. "Only, you'll have to try to be nice to the others, Tania. Let's not have any hair-pulling!"

"Hmm! I don't promise anything. If I see one of them playing up to you, I'll scratch her eyes out! Just let them remember that!"

Eventually, she decided to relax her passionate hold on him and Bernard was able to breathe a little more freely. It was then he noticed, to his great surprise, that his tender Tania was sumptuously dressed in a robe that was completely alien to a planet of the Fortrun empire.

"Good Lord!" exclaimed the general. "That's the kind of thing they wear in the imperial court. How on earth did you ever get hold of it?"

The beautiful Russian was indeed decked out in a long yellow velvet robe and train embroidered with gold. It had short bouffant sleeves and a deep décolletage that exposed a good portion of her voluptuous breasts..

"*Chéri*, it was that darling Ar'zog who gave it to me, but please don't be jealous! I told him that we wanted to celebrate your return. He thought that was very amusing, and he gave us whatever we wanted. He rummaged through the memories of your doubles, and his robots sewed up these magnificent gowns for us. You know, as the consort of General Bernard I'm somebody now, and I can't just go around in a peasant dress. Do you like it?"

"Of course! You look wonderful. I never thought to see you this way, but that gown suits you just fine."

"I've also got some jewels."

"So I see. An emerald necklace and some extraordinary rings. Ar'zog really does things in grand style!"

"Maybe now you'll be willing to marry me?" ·

The question took the general by surprise and he stammered: "My God, I never really thought about it before. Aren't you happy as you are?"

Tania pouted sadly and seemed very disappointed.

"Don't you think I'm pretty enough? Or is it that you don't want to lower yourself by marrying a peasant?"

The poor girl seemed almost on the point of tears. Fearing a scene, the general quickly protested:

"Not at all! On the contrary, I'd be delighted to marry you. The only thing is, the marriage would have absolutely no validity, as there is no priest among us and no civilian authority such as we know it on Earth."

"Bah! What difference does that make? We're no longer living on that planet. Ar'zog promised we could have a ceremony of some kind. Anyhow, all your friends will be getting married too! You see, I've thought of everything!"

Once more the officer could think of nothing to say. No doubt about it, women had strange notions! Imagine wanting a formal wedding under such circumstances. Here they were, an immeasurable distance from the Earth, and right in the middle of a galactic war! A glance around him, however, confirmed what Tania had said: all the Russian women, dressed in court robes and clinging to the arm of the colonel of their choice, were coming toward him.

"Well, if it will give you any pleasure, I agree," he stammered. "When shall the wedding be?"

"Right now, darling! Don't worry, I've seen to everything, and I even have a little surprise for you."

By this time very little could have surprised Bernard.

He took his place at the head of the cortege, and the couples moved off to a waiting hovercar, which took off immediately and a few minutes later arrived at its destination. The men were not yet fully aware of what was happening to them.

The hovercar landed on a carefully tended lawn ornamented by expertly trimmed clumps of shrubbery. A magnificent white stone building stood before the amazed eyes of the new arrivals.

"Why, that's Malmaison, the home of the Empress Josephine," Bernard said in a strangled voice. "I recognize the rose garden and the Marengo cedar. How can it be possible?"

"But, *chéri*, you know very well that the Fortruns are real magicians! You had once visited this château, and all they had to do was search your memory. The robots did the rest. Unfortunately, you had never seen more than the ground-floor rooms. When it came to the bedrooms we had to improvise a bit, but the results are rather smart and I hope you'll like it. Hurry along now, they're waiting for us."

Robot footmen in livery bowed as the important guests went up the little stone terrace and began inspecting the place, proceeding from surprise to surprise. They passed in succession through the combined study-library whose shelves were heavy with innumerable, expensively bound books with pages innocent of any printed matter. Behind some of the books were psychic tapes and projection equipment. Next, the soldiers and their ladies went into the Council Room, where they admired a tentlike decor and martial motifs. In the dining room a complete service of porcelain and vermeil dishes was displayed on the buffet and the serving tables, but the initials had been changed and modified so that each dish boasted a *B* surrounded by bees.

The billard room brought cries of pleasure from the men, who were delighted to come across an entertainment they had enjoyed during their long garrison years. They could already foresee many happy sessions here. The floor was covered with a Savonnerie carpet bearing Bernard's initial.

Finally, they reached the reception room. There a buffet awaited them. Liveried robots did the honors. Through the open door one could see the music room and the numerous instruments, especially a marvelous harp. Pictures covered the walls of the largest room—portraits of all the soldiers and their future wives in the style of the painter Gérard.

"Well, my friend," said Faultrier coming up to the couple. "This can really be called a surprise! What a sly one you are! You might at least have told *me*!"

"With all respect, General," added Géraudont, "it's just what I imagined Paradise would be like!"

"Yes," said Chastel, his eyes wide with amazement. "I have never seen anything so beautiful."

"So this is where the Little Corporal kept house with his Josephine. He could certainly never have been bored *here*," Bourief chimed in enthusiastically.

"Is this where we're going to live from now on?" asked Queunot. "If the people back home could see me now, they wouldn't believe their eyes! Cousin Loïc would be green with envy. 'You'll never amount to much,' he used to say. Well, my fine friend, if you only knew!"

The general was beginning to get a grip on himself. Raising his hand, he called for silence and said coolly enough:

"Don't get so excited, my friends! We'll do even better than this, I promise you. But before going any further, I want to make an important announcement. This joyous day is my wedding day. I am marrying Tania!"

"Long live General Bernard! Long life and prosperity to him! Long live the bride!" shouted the soldiers in an attempt to outdo one another as they unsheathed their sabers.

"Obviously I'm not going to be the only groom, since you, too, have chosen your hearts' elect, and if I may say so, it appears that we are all to take this happy step simultaneously. May you have many children and always be very happy! However, I hope that the charms of our beautiful companions will not make you forget our mission here. The Kveyars must be swept from this galactic sector!"

The robot-footmen now advanced and served cups of a bubbling topaz liquid, a synthetic champagne that enchanted the palates of these connoisseurs. Then Ar'zog made his entrance.

An orchestra made up of instruments of the kind they had on Earth struck up a lively tune, and the Fortrun mounted a small platform and began a little speech—a telepathic one, of course.

"My dear allies, we are happy to have been able to give you these little trinkets as an expression of our gratitude. The custom of your country demands that those who want to procreate make a solemn exchange of rings. This must certainly signify an indestructible union. Well, since you will have it so, let us proceed to the ceremony."

Chapter Nine

Looking solemn, as is only proper in such circumstances, the Earthlings took the arms of their future spouses—the ladies' fathers regretfully not being present to escort them—and lined up in twos behind their leader. With martial step they moved toward the officiant and stopped before him.

Bernard and Tania, somewhat at sea and not knowing how this unusual ceremony would proceed, decided to kneel and wait to see what would happen.

The Fortrun came up to them and asked simply:

"Tania Voribova, do you take General Bernard for your husband?"

"I do," whispered the young woman.

"General Bernard, do you take Tania Voribova for your wife?"

"I do!" said the Frenchman in a clear voice.

"I therefore declare you united by the bonds of matrimony. May I be the first to congratulate you! General, as an expression of our esteem for you, and since such seems to be the custom in your country, I confer on you the title of Duke of Ariman, along with all the prerogatives attached to such a title on Earth. Upon its liberation, you will be the sovereign of that stellar sector."

His surprise was such that the general could only splutter:

"Me, a duke? You do me too much honor."

Inviting the new noble and his bride to stand alongside him, Ar'zog began to perform the same ceremony for the other officers. He did not, however, ennoble them, leaving this for Bernard to do later, according to their merits.

Each couple received a parchment testifying to their

104

marriage, then the Fortrun discreetly slipped away so that his allies would be free to celebrate among themselves.

The orchestra struck up a wedding march while the officers were congratulating one another. They all came to bow before the General-Duke of Ariman, and Faultrier, very moved, stammered:

"Your Majesty, Your Grace ... *sacrénom*, I'm not sure what to call you now!"

"Come, come," said Bernard with a laugh, "there's no need for ceremony between old friends."

"Ah! Well, that suits me fine. All my best wishes to you and your charming wife. I hope that she will soon have need for my services—to bring your descendants into the world, I mean," he said with a laugh, as Tania blushed.

"Congratulations to you, too. I'm sure that Katia will be a tender and faithful wife. I don't know a thing about my duchy, but I promise to assign you a planet of your own choosing and to confer on you the title of count. Your descendants will establish themselves there, and you can devote yourself to their education in all tranquility as soon as we have finished off the Kveyars!"

"Let's not talk about the war," interrupted Tania. "Let's just forget it so that it won't ruin this day. Come and dance. We are to open the ball. You'll see, thanks to the Fortruns, I've learned the mazurka, the gaillarde, and even the gavotte."

Bernard gallantly gave his arm to the lovely Tania, the others took their places, the robot-orchestra struck up a lively mazurka, and all the couples began to dance.

But a surprise awaited them. The dance floor had been equipped with an anti-g mechanism, so that the dancers were all but weightless and were soon swirling above the ground in graceful arabesques. The Russian women had had time to practice, and they spun about in the air with undisguised pleasure, but it took the men a little while to familiarize themselves with this new way of dancing.

However, they got the hang of it quickly enough, and soon the room resounded with the laughter and pleasantries of these lusty fellows whose temperaments were in no way inclined to melancholy.

They were even quite delighted with the fact that in the course of their swirling and turning the robes of the ladies floated upward to reveal lacy and beribboned undergarments.

The evening passed in such unrestrained joy, and the synthetic champagne flowed so freely, that when Bernard left the ballroom to ascend to his apartments, several of the gentlemen had a great deal of difficulty in following him.

Géraudont, in particular, clamored for the reestablishment of normal gravity, since his sense of balance left much to be desired. As for Kaninski, his Slav temperament got the upper hand and he wept bitter tears as he listened to Lisa wring heartbreaking notes from a balalaika borrowed from one of the robots in the orchestra.

The evening had been a memorable one, but the General-Duke of Ariman was still in for some surprises. When Tania opened the door of the nuptial chamber, he emitted a strangled cry:

"Ah! Good God!"

"What is it, *chéri*?" his gentle wife asked in astonishment. "Don't you like the way it's decorated? Ar'zog assured me that it was the exact reproduction of a place in which you used to enjoy yourself enormously."

Bernard contemplated the wainscoting, the walls covered with sparkling mirrors that reflected every image into infinity, the enormous four-poster bed with transparent hangings, and then he said:

"And he was very right, my love. I spent some delightful hours in a room just like this, but for a moment I was a little surprised. . . ."

And he thought to himself: *Surprised is hardly the word for it! The fanciest cathouse in Smolensk! It's a lucky thing I wear this net these days! This kind of meddling in my thoughts will end by stirring up*

*trouble. . . . Never mind—the decor is just right for the
business at hand!*

And he swiftly and expertly undid the robe of his
companion.

The night was spent in the delights of the marriage
bed, but even the best things must come to an end, and
when the officers met with their leader the next day,
rather late in the morning, he immediately got down to
cases.

The general allowed them to settle comfortably into
the armchairs of the study-library and then declared:

"My friends, I'm probably going to sound like a kill-
joy to you, but we absolutely must not allow ourselves
to be made as soft as the Fortruns by the pleasures
available to us. We have a sumptuous residence and
charming wives, and this may disincline us to combat
the Kveyars. Nevertheless, we must not forget that
these warlike creatures are threatening to invade
Dumyat. I got up early this morning, and while I was
strolling around the grounds I was able to think out a
plan for our coming campaign. Ar'zog has promised to
multiply our troops tenfold. This means we will have
twenty artillery batteries and thirty infantry companies.
That's enough to plan a fight on a considerably increased scale. In addition, one hundred spaceships are
waiting at the astroport. Half of them are armed cargo
vessels needed for troop transportation; the rest are
ships equipped with powerful armament. Our objective
will be Usk. You probably know nothing about the
place, so I'm going to give you a few pointers.

"The Uskians are people who are very much like
us—physically, at least. This is true to such an extent
that at one point the Fortruns thought to find in them
the military leaders they needed. Their civilization is
relatively primitive, though they are considerably more
evolved than the people on Earth. They are experts in
the art of composing poems and songs, and their music
is said to be remarkable. Many of the colorful paintings
you've been admiring were created by their artists.

"On the other hand, their industry is all but nonexis-
tent; Usk has no significant mineral resources. In other

words, it does not constitute a valuable strategic objective, especially since it is all the way on the right wing of the present front. You all know my method by this time: attack where the enemy computers least expect it. To confuse our enemies still further, an airfleet will take off just before we do and head directly for the principal Kveyar base. Actually, the fleet will consist of only a few ships towing decoys—hollow shells made of inflatable metalized plastic, which the Kveyar detectors will mistake for spaceships.

"While this is going on, we will be quietly heading for our real objective. There are a few enemy squadrons in the vicinity, but they will be unable to receive reinforcements in time. I might add that the Uskians allowed the Kveyars to occupy their planet without offering any resistance. Obviously, then, we cannot count on their help."

"Isn't it dangerous to leave Dumyat so unprotected?" objected Friancourt.

"I admit I'm running a risk. But remember that the enemy computers are going to try to figure out what happened at Oloch. They must certainly suspect the presence of Fortrun allies behind their lines. I have consulted our own computers and find that in a similar situation they would dispatch a strong patrol to the Oloch sector before launching an attack. Just about the time they discover they've drawn a blank, the news of our arrival in Usk will reach them, and they will speed off in that new direction. The only thing is, the reinforcements will not arrive until after the battle is over!"

"What about the Uskians?" asked Faultrier. "Can we count on them? Isn't there some risk that they may betray us?"

"Peaceable humanoids who are courageous but accustomed to living in idyllic comfort thanks to Fortrun subsidies cannot ally themselves with cruel savages like the Kveyars! Besides, the fact that they resemble us will be of enormous help when we make our initial contact with them."

"How many ships do our enemies have available?" asked Kaninski at this point.

"They have barely a hundred in this sector."

"Not to be sneezed at, if the swine know how to fight!" grumbled Chastel.

"We mustn't overestimate them. The officers commanding these forces have never been in combat. The seasoned troops are assigned elsewhere."

"Can we see what these Uskians look like?" asked Géraudont.

"Certainly."

Bernard got a projector down from the library shelves and inserted a slide. A couple who could easily be mistaken for Earthlings materialized in the middle of the room.

"Pretty girl!" noted Bourief. "I'd much rather deal with these people than with the horrors we've met until now!"

"Venetian blond hair," added Queunot. "My dream!"

"That's enough, you bunch of lechers!" interrupted the general-duke. "You seem to forget that you've just been officially married! Any other questions?"

Nobody spoke. Bernard replaced the projector and continued:

"Well, all we have to do is embark. I'll give you ten minutes to say your good-byes to your wives. We'll assemble at the astroport."

The separation was touching, and several of the young women broke into sobs on learning that their husbands were going to leave them so soon after the wedding. They had to resign themselves to it, however, since there was no hope for a normal life until the Kveyar menace had been definitively removed.

When the Earthmen arrived at the astroport the troops had already been loaded on, for the general was in a hurry to reach his destination and feared that the Kveyars might attempt to intercept his armies. Only Ar'zog was there waiting for them.

"General," he declared, "I wish you luck on your undertaking. You certainly have curious methods, but the results seem to bear you out. I am therefore giving you carte blanche, as I promised. And in order to show just how much we value you, we have arranged a surprise:

you were afraid that your headquarters group was not large enough for your increased forces. Well, I think that problem has been resolved. . . ."

Just then Bernard saw the orderly approach of a troop; the sight made him cry out in surprise: seventy-two human soldiers, each original having been duplicated in nine exact copies!

"Of course," continued the Fortrun, "each of your doubles is conditioned to remain subject to the orders of the original; thus there is no question of precedence, and the problem of the command of your new regiments has been resolved."

Then he discreetly slipped away and left the twin brothers confronting one another.

"A rather curious feeling," Faultrier confided to his friend.

"Yes," agreed Bernard, still hypnotized by the spectacle. "Down deep I was expecting it, but still, it really does something to you to find yourself suddenly the oldest brother in a large family! How am I going to know which is which?"

"The simplest thing is to give them a number. You will be number one, and so on down the line. . . ."

"Sacrénom! I wonder if I'll ever get used to it!"

One after another, the officers met their brothers. The resemblance was so striking they would have sworn they were looking into mirrors, but the newcomers seemed very untroubled by the meeting. It posed no problems for them: they accepted the rights of seniority and it never occurred to them to question the supremacy of the firstborn.

Bernard soon got over his surprise. To emphasize the hierarchy of his new headquarters staff, he immediately gave himself the title of marshal, and promoted his original comrades to the rank of general. The "brothers" were all made colonels. As the Fortruns had equipped the products of their incubators with a memory that included all the elements of the original on which they were modeled, there was no need for any training sessions.

The Marshal-Duke of Ariman therefore gave the

110

order to embark. The generals accompanied him onto the *Victory of Friedland*. As for the colonels, they rejoined their regiments.

Immediately after the squadron's departure, a message was received in which Ar'zog wished them good luck on their expedition and explained that to avoid marital problems the incubators had provided each of the doubles with a bride. He also advised them that the "Faultriers and Géraudonts" of the new series had received a training somewhat different from their originals and were able to assume military commands. Only the "Number Ones" would remain with the medical corps.

Bernard thanked him and, entering his cabin, began to think over the coming campaign.

He was very troubled by the sudden appearance of the doubles. Had the Fortruns, as skilled psychologists, meant to create rivals for him? Surely if his brothers resembled him in every way, they, too, must be possessed of boundless ambition. Wouldn't they try to take his place? True, the problem had been somewhat defused by making them subordinate to his original companions, whose fidelity was unconditional, but he'd nevertheless have to keep an eye on them.

Fortunately the doubles were not equipped with thought-nets and so could be spied on while they slept. At the first suspicious sign, his brothers would have to be pitilessly liquidated—and after all, what could be easier than to destroy a ship in the midst of a battle once you knew its exact position?

Reassured on this point, the marshal-duke began to consider a second problem, a strategic one this time. The marvelous relief maps he was able to make materialize inside a globe allowed him to form a very exact idea of the future stellar battlefields.

His attention was immediately drawn by an enormous nebula in front of his objective. His adversaries would surely try to give battle there, for it offered the advantage of protecting their flank. The intense energy fields within the nebula made it impossible to traverse, except at its periphery where the arms of ionized material must be thinner.

Just to make sure, Bernard consulted his private computer, which confirmed his opinion. He would have to study this zone carefully so as to wring maximum profit from its shape.

For several hours the marshal worked out his battle plan. The tele-radars of the lead units kept furnishing him with up-to-the-minute information on the forces confronting them, and it soon became obvious that the combat would be on more or less equal terms, since the Kveyars were beginning to become aware of the objective of the enemy vessels and were concentrating all their available ships in the Usk planet sector.

Time passed, and nobody dared disturb Bernard, who remained isolated in his cabin. He had, as a matter of fact, given strict orders on this subject, even if it were one of his own brothers—of whom he was greatly suspicious—who should want to see him. Not fully trusting them, he tended to consider these brothers as spies in the pay of the Fortruns.

However, the first of the advance guard skirmishes soon occurred and it was necessary to speak to the marshal. Faultrier offered to do so and came to knock at the cabin door. He received a gruff invitation to enter.

"Well, old warrior?" exclaimed the surgeon. "Have you lost interest in our enemies? The Kveyars are beginning to fire on our lead ships."

"I know. The central information post feeds into the equipment in my cabin. The shipboard computer has my instructions. For the moment there's nothing for me to do."

"What's this? You're leaving control of the operation to this mechanical gadget? I thought you wanted to do just the opposite—that you wanted to take action that would be completely unpredictable!"

"Of course! But only when it's a question of choosing the objective or of determining where I'm going to apply pressure during a battle. The rest of the time it's important that our enemies believe that everything is going on as usual."

"Oh, I see. Well, that's reassuring. I thought for a moment that you had changed your mind."

"You don't have to worry. I have more reason than ever to finish this business as soon as possible—I don't want your wives to curse me! Here, see for yourself what Usk looks like."

He pointed to a screen on which they could see a very ordinary-looking yellowish planet. On its left stretched a vast nebula formed of ionized gases twisting in thick swirls. From a distance it looked like a large, luminous spider web. The *Victory of Friedland* had already passed its outer edge and was now moving alongside a reddish arm that looked like a tongue of fire darting out of a furnace.

"Brr!" said Faultrier. "I wouldn't like to plunge into that!"

"No. And that's exactly why our enemies, operating on orders from their computers, are going to try to back us up against the nebula. But I have a surprise in store for them. Do you see those green points?"

"Yes, three groups toward the front."

"They are enemy squadrons. Ours appear as orange spots. We should make contact somewhere near the long-drawn-out arm just in front of Usk. Their plan is simple. Two armies of the left wing that are right off the nebula are first going to try to halt us; then they will attempt to outflank me and cut me off in the rear. While they're doing this the third group will follow along the nebula and try to infiltrate to seal off the pocket behind us. Caught between two fires like that, we'd be in a sorry position!"

"That's a nice state of affairs! An attack on both flanks to form a pocket in which we'll be trapped like rats! It's classic, but dangerous. How do you intend to go about circumventing this plan?"

"It's very simple. According to the computers, I should grapple on to the two wings in order to contain them, especially in the most dangerous sector: the nebula. Actually, I've decided to take somewhat different action. My forces will be separated into four armies. My left wing, the one farthest from the ionized gases, is reinforced and is not to give way by so much as an inch. However, on the right I've given orders for a flabby defense and for a retreat to be made along the impenetrable gaseous arms.

"While this is happening, I go over to the offensive in the center and push their two armies against the nebula. They will have to fight with their backs against this trap, in which dangerous spatial distortions make all navigation impossible. We will easily be able to destroy them."

"*My God,* that seems like a good idea! We'll see if things work out as you've planned. But what if anything goes wrong, and we have to go through those furious atoms? It gives me the chills just to think of it! I would obviously have made a very poor soldier and an aboslutely terrible general. You have to have nerves of steel under all circumstances. . . ."

"Now, now, don't get yourself all worked up. Take a seat, have a drink, and watch that screen as though it were some kind of dramatic spectacle. For the moment, I don't have any more time for you."

Faultrier poured himself a generous portion and settled into his armchair, admiring his friend's calm.

For three long hours a ferocious struggle took place near the nebula. As Bernard had foreseen, the Kveyars resolutely attacked on both flanks. On the left of the screen, Friancourt, faced with forces stronger than his own, accomplished miracles and managed to hold his positions. As the other end, Queunot, following his orders, fell back as he fiercely fought along the arm of the nebula; then he halted his ships and courageously stood his ground.

At that point, Bernard and Kaninski launched their forces against the center, the very point at which they had more spaceships than the enemy. The armament on both sides was almost equal, but since the events at Oloch, the Kveyars were leery of a trap and held back.

The two Fortrun squadrons were therefore able to carry out the planned maneuver, quickly swinging around toward the nebula on to the enemy's rear. Two

Kveyar squadrons fell into the trap and were decimated under the furious charges of the marshal-duke's troops.

Suddenly, Queunot went over to a counterattack. More than half the enemy ships were destroyed; some twenty others, disabled, surrendered. Only a few tried to flee by slipping into the gaseous whirlpools, and very few of those survived.

Realizing what was happening, the Kveyars fighting against Friancourt broke off combat and went to the aid of the other two squadrons. But the light cavalry kept on their heels, and then Kaninski's spaceships did a sudden turnabout so that their backs were to the nebula. Once again the Kveyars were caught between two lines of fire. They soon realized their situation was hopeless and the leaders fled as quickly as they could, drawing away from Usk and leaving the robots to manage for themselves. Without anyone to give them orders, however, the mechanical men were quickly put out of action.

The battle was over. Three-quarters of the enemy's forces had been liquidated. As for the commander of the sector, he was still trying to figure out what had happened to him! Hadn't he followed to the letter the orders of the previously infallible computers?

"Damn!" exclaimed Faultrier, who had by then emptied about a third of the bottle of synthetic rum in order to keep his spirits up. "Well, old chum, you certainly know how to go about things! I would bet that even the Little Corporal could not have done better. And yet ... somehow the maneuver seems very familiar to me. . . ."

"Of course it does!" said Bernard, exploding with laughter. "You remember Austerlitz, I suppose? Actually, all I did was adapt what happened there. The nebula was the equivalent of the Telnitz 'lakes' and that's how the trap was sprung."

Chapter Ten

Faithful to the Napoleonic tradition, the marshal-duke congratulated his troops on their courageous behavior during the battle. The "brothers" had fought valiantly, scrupulously obeying his orders and showing no inclination toward independence.

In full lyric flow, Bernard finished his talk by assuring them: "You will only have to say: 'I was at Usk' for people to respond: 'There's a brave man for you!'"

That done, he saluted, as his officers who had come aboard the *Victory of Friedland* for the ceremony cheered, and withdrew to get some rest. But fate had otherwise decreed. He had scarcely reached his cabin when he was recalled to the command post.

The Uskians were signaling for help. The message was retransmitted to him, and to his great surprise, a ravishing female form appeared on the screen. What she had to say quickly explained the reason for her anguished appeal.

"Thank you from the bottom of my heart for having liberated us from the yoke of the Kveyars, Your Excellency," she declared. "I am Hina, daughter of the ruler of this planet. My father was killed by the brutes before they fled, and the demons have launched the black death against us. Come to our aid quickly, or we will all perish."

Bernard turned to his friend Faultrier.

"Do you know what she means?"

"Yes," the surgeon replied immediately. "She's talking about a form of bacteriological warfare. The spore of a mushroom is used to contaminate the human organism, either by attacking the respiratory system or by a simple attack on the skin. The entire body is very

116

quickly invaded and each cell transformed into black spores. Soon there is only ebony dust under a parchmented skin, and the poor wretches who have caught this plague die after atrocious suffering. The Uskian settlements are under protective globes, so the Kveyars must have polluted them by using the air distribution and climate control system."

"What can be done?"

"Spacesuits are good protection against it. Certain kinds of masks may work, if impermeable plastic clothing is also worn. Once the epidemic has broken out, you have to use fungicides, either by way of aerosol sprays or in the form of pills that can be taken orally."

"Do we have any on board?"

"Yes, of course, but not in sufficient quantity."

Bernard thought for a moment as he contemplated the anguished face of the beautiful young woman who was awaiting his decision; then he said in his usual dynamic manner:

"Head for Usk! Twenty ships are to escort us. Kaninski, you take command of the fleet and return to Dumyat. After the beating they've just received, I don't think the Kveyars will venture back into this sector, but they may very well turn their attention to the Fortruns. If there are any suspicious enemy movements, let me know immediately."

The hussar saluted and left the ship to execute his leader's orders. The other officers followed suit. Only Faultrier remained with the marshal-duke.

"All right," Bernard said to the beautiful Uskian, "we're coming as quickly as possible. In the meantime, tell me what happened."

"Oh, it was the usual technique. With unscrupulous creatures such as these, one has to expect anything. One day, about six months ago, a Kveyar ambassador came to see my father.

" 'It seems to us that your people may have need of protection against the Fortruns,' declared the wretch. 'We are therefore resolved to lend you troops to defend your planet, which seems to be very backward in military matters. There will be spaceship bases on Usk,

117

and we will launch defense satellites into orbit to spot any potential aggressor. Of course, we will have to ask you for a reasonable contribution toward the expense of maintaining these forces.'

"My father immediately understood the implied threat. 'At least be frank about it,' he replied. 'The fact of the matter is that you want to annex Usk and draw subsidies from it. I warn you that mine is a peace-loving people whose only interest is in arts and letters. Our factories produce only what we need to live on, and we have no war fleet.' But the Kveyar replied: 'It doesn't matter. I know that your people are devoted to pointless amusements, but I also know that they are intelligent and skillful. We are going to change things and convert these lazy fellows. From now on, they will work at perfecting the precision equipment needed by our spaceships. That's how they will pay their way.'

"What could my father do? He was powerless to prevent his people from being reduced to slavery, so he accepted the Kveyar occupation without putting up a struggle. A secret appeal was sent to the Fortruns, but they had no means by which to oppose the Kveyar armies. We had to resign ourselves to the law of the strongest. Our lovely countryside had been deformed by the construction of arms factories, and my compatriots have had to leave their beloved music and painting to work for the occupying power.

"Then we learned that a great battle would take place near Usk. Ships kept landing to be supplied and then hurtling back into the sky. When we saw this imposing display of Kveyar strength, our hopes of liberation quickly vanished. Nobody could ever conquer such an army! And then our prayers were miraculously answered. Suddenly the occupiers boarded their ships and fled in haste. When we picked up the news of your victory, how happy we were.... Alas! a horrible fate lay in store for us: the black death! More than a third of my people have caught it.

"Who are you, you who so much resemble us and whose bravery is equaled only by your beauty? I didn't

118

know there was a race like our own in this sector of the galaxy."

Flattered, Bernard proudly replied: "Don't be afraid. A fast ship will bring the medicines you need from Dumyat. Meanwhile, we will use what we have on board the ships here.

"Allow me to present myself. I am Marshal Bernard, Duke of Ariman. Earth is our planet of origin, and it is in what you call the Ednar constellation. My people have only a primitive civilization and don't even know the secret of atomic energy, but the Fortruns felt that we could give them invaluable aid. It is quite true that we on Earth have had centuries of battle experience, and thus we possess a knowledge of war that the Fortruns lack completely. That's why they asked Earthlings to take over the command of their armed forces and fight the Kveyars. The man alongside me is my friend Faultrier; he is a doctor and in charge of the army medical services. He was trained by the Fortruns and knows all about their medical discoveries. I am certain he will soon find a way to stamp out this epidemic."

"Do what you can quickly, I beg you," pleaded the sovereign of Usk, wringing her hands in anguish. "The plague is spreading from minute to minute."

"We will be with you in half an hour at the most. Transmit a signal to guide us in. Courage!"

The gentle face vanished from the screen.

His brows knit, the marshal-duke remained plunged in thought. The victory he had just won would give the Kveyars much to think about, especially since their computer had been in error. They would then proceed to a logical examination of the affair. A search would be made for the errors committed in the course of the battle, and they would have no trouble finding many of them. Next the Kveyar computers would be reprogrammed with fresh instructions that would take into account the newly acquired experience. The important thing, then, was to take action at the next battle that would again be the contrary of what their electronic brains told them would happen. However, there seemed little chance that the Kveyars would risk another battle in the immediate future. They needed time to resolve this problem and to build up sufficient forces. It was therefore possible to stay a while on Usk and attempt to save as many people as possible.

Was it perhaps their great resemblance to humans that urged him to take a personal interest in this affair, which could very well have been handled by Queunot? Or was it perhaps the sad smile of Hina that had weighed so heavily in his decision?

"Do you think we have a chance of saving them?" he abruptly asked his friend.

"So you've suddenly become concerned about the fate of your fellow man, have you?" jested Faultrier. "Well, to be frank, many of these good people are going to die. The spores have had time to introduce themselves everywhere, and we will need large quantities of disinfectant to get them under control. As for the oral fungicide, our stock is only large enough to give emergency treatment to the most important people on Usk. They have every chance of getting well; the antidote the Fortruns have developed against the black death is remarkably effective."

"Can we visit them?"

"Yes, if we make sure that we don't take off our protective suits, which will be carefully disinfected in a sealed chamber on our return to Dumyat. As an extra precaution, we will also have to take a dose of oral fungicide."

"Are their cities permanently uninhabitable?"

"Their cities are all under globes. Infection by means of the air-conditioning system was therefore simple, but by the same token the spores were unable to spread over the surface of the planet. It will be relatively easy to rid the Uskians of these deadly germs by using the aerosol fungicides, but we won't be able to do that until we receive sufficient supplies from Dumyat."

"Fine! I'm counting on you. Do your best. These people strike me as being extremely sympathetic, and I would like to make allies of them."

"Leave it to me! But I feel you are taking an unnecessary risk by landing on Usk."

"That's my business. They'll remember that gesture. I need some devoted friends in this strange world. The Uskians can be useful."

Shortly after this exchange, the *Victory of Friedland* landed on the liberated planet. Bernard and his friends could see for themselves that the reputation of its inhabitants had in no way been exaggerated. Never had they seen such beautiful landscapes.

The countryside was nothing less than an immense garden in which the essences of all growing things mingled in perfect harmony. The eye was enchanted by marvelously colored flowers. The crystal rocks themselves were used to vary the decor, and mineral clusters lit by invisible sources of light threw off sparkling fires that made the dazzling corollas pale beside them. Graceful animals, birds with multicolored plumage, insects with diaphanous wings—all added to the splendor of this idyllic spot.

In some places, mobiles or statues—works of artistic genius in veritable open-air museums—attracted the eye, infinitely varying the themes with incredible imagination.

Usk was truly the jewel of the galaxy, the fruit of a refined civilization which had for centuries been working to place all the resources of technique in the service of art, and doing it so subtly that some of its achievements seemed the work of nature alone.

Of course the charm of music was not overlooked either, and melodious symphonies were carried on the soft breezes.

The Kveyar occupation had, however, taken its toll. In some places on these wonderful landscapes, purely military constructions massacred the immense garden perspectives. Happily, these spots were rare, the factories generally having been built underground for security reasons.

The capital of Usk, metropolis of all the arts, was also an incomparable jewel, each building giving its inhabitants the opportunity to exhibit new artistic skills.

Pierre Barbet

The ensemble formed a gigantic relief-painting in sumptuous shades.

From the very beginning of the epidemic it had been forbidden to enter or leave the cities. The exterior remained healthy, and under no circumstances was a general pollution of the planet to be risked. The lucky ones who happened to be in the open air remained healthy, but those who found themselves trapped under the domes were the prey of the plague. Guards in protective suits had to watch over the air locks and the sides of the globe, since the unfortunates, ready to do anything to get out, kept rushing with whatever tools they could get their hands on to the transparent walls that imprisoned them.

Bernard and Faultrier, accompanied by a squad of some fifty robots, entered the city and saw the bodies of those luckless ones who had had to be slain to prevent them from escaping. The guards pitilessly shot down any citizen who came closer than twenty meters to the edge of the city. Electronic paralyzing barriers had been established, but in the wild hope of escaping this death-trap some of the inhabitants attempted to cross by driving through them in transport vehicles moving at top speed.

Anti-gs traveling a few meters above the ground brought the Earthlings to the seat of the government, which was surrounded by a powerful protective shield. As they passed through the city they could see the effects of the black death; the cremation crews had been unable to keep up with their task and bodies lay strewn about the streets and gardens.

All the corpses had parchmented skin, as though it had dried up, and through splits one could see the interior of the body, which had been reduced to a powdery magma that spread like a sooty dust at the least breath of wind.

Some of those infected were still alive and they staggered about. Their epidermis looked like punk and kept peeling off in carbonaceous flakes.

As the vehicles passed, a few people stretched out their arms in a plea for help. The Earthlings noticed

122

with horror that the eyes of these Uskians were no more than tarry orbs from which flowed tears the color of ink.

"How horrible!" exclaimed Bernard. "I can understand fighting with equal arms in space or elsewhere, but these Kveyars are contemptible to have used such means against defenseless civilians!"

"I'm not the one to contradict you," agreed the surgeon, nodding his head. "War is horrible enough on Earth, but highly technological civilizations have very terrifying weapons. And our struggle against the Kveyars is nowhere near over. You've launched a frightening venture, and I wonder how it will all end."

The marshal did not reply; nothing could alter his decision. This vast universe with its planets, its riches, would never belong to the Kveyars. He had been torn from his subordinate position and given the taste for power, and now he swore to become the uncontested master of this gigantic empire.

A few minutes later the hovercar and its escort stopped before an imposing building surrounded by armed robots. Bernard and Faultrier got out of the vehicle and penetrated the entry lock, from which they came out onto a vast hall decorated with profusion of statues and bas-reliefs. It looked like a museum, but it was only an ordinary theater that had been taken over because it was large enough to shelter essential government services.

Hina and several notables awaited them. After having been disinfected, the Earthlings swallowed a few doses of fungicide. The robots then began to distribute the precious medical supplies to the Uskians present.

The young woman before them was quite splendid, and the marshal felt that he had never before come across such perfect beauty. By comparison, Tania was completely unattractive. What struck him most was the regal bearing, the innate majesty that showed she had the habit of ruling and of confronting problems.

The trial she was undergoing seemed to have left no mark on her, though she risked a horrible death at any moment. She appeared neither fearful nor depressed.

123

"Thank you, Earthlings, for having so quickly come to our aid! In this way we will be able to save at least some of my unfortunate subjects. Tell me what is to be done. Every Uskian is at your orders, and their princess will always remember those who scorned all dangers and came as saviors."

"Madame," replied the marshal, "the most elementary charity demanded that we liberate a people whose marvelous achievements are an honor to civilization. Our similar physical natures make me feel that for the first time I am again among people like myself. Everything will therefore be done to wipe out the plague that has struck you. For the time being we must limit the distribution of medicine to those of your subjects who are in the most urgent need. In two days we will have sufficient supplies for everybody. Meanwhile, my friend Faultrier will help your public health services take whatever steps are called for by the emergency. I wanted to come to you in person, despite the demands upon me, to assure you of all my sympathy and of my firm support. As long as I am alive, the Kveyars will never again ravage this planet!"

"Have you then received orders to war against these scavengers?" Hina asked earnestly. "It is a glorious mission, but also a heavy responsibility. According to the reports I have received, your victory in the recent battle was complete. Until now nobody has ever been able to fight off these pillagers! The name of Marshal Bernard will remain in our annals forever. Your bravery explains many things, but have you no other secrets?"

"We Earthlings are primitives who are very undeveloped in many domains when compared with the peoples of this galaxy. We have not yet arrived at a stage that would permit us to play a role in your stellar federation. Long years of struggle, however, have at least taught us how to fight for survival. Technology cannot replace everything. The methods employed in our world are evidently efficient, and that's my whole secret."

"You also seem to know how to hold your tongue,"

commented Hina with a smile. "That's only right, since your conceptions of the arts of war are no concern of mine. Still, isn't it to be feared that the Kveyars will call in some of your comrades to direct their armies?"

"They don't so much as suspect our existence, and I think that the Uskians will know how to be discreet on this point. But even supposing that such were to happen someday, there's no reason to assume that my techniques won't be up to that of the newcomers."

"You've worked out an entirely new strategy," noted the princess. "I can only admire you the more for it, since the machines used by the Kveyars and the Fortruns have been perfected to a high degree. However, I don't want to appear indiscreet. My gratitude and that of my people are yours forever. You've given us a lesson that I hope we will remember. If one is to survive, it's not enough to live in peace and devote oneself to the arts and the cultivation of the spirit. An unarmed people is always a tempting prey for the unscrupulous. We must therefore learn the art of war from you. As soon as the plague has been brought under control, I will ask that you accept some Uskians as observers so that they can be trained in your methods."

"I will receive them with pleasure," the marshal assured her. "But make no mistake about it. Long years of practice are necessary before perfection in this domain can be achieved. The emperor of my people, Napoleon, is an excellent example of this. I merely follow his teachings; on Earth I had only a modest rank in his army."

"The greater my admiration for you! It must take exceptional qualities to be able to transfer to spaceships a strategy designed for ground combat. May success continue to crown all your efforts! But I keep you here talking and make you lose precious time. Know that we are very sensible of the honor you have paid us in coming to Usk in person when such a heavy task lies before you. The enemy forces are enormous and you will have to fight many battles to conquer them. Before you go, I would like to express our gratitude by bestowing upon you our highest decoration, one reserved for our princes and our most eminent artists: the Seven-Pointed Shining Star."

Upon these words, Hina took a wonderful medal from a case. From its center a topaz shot off seven rays whose splendor made the light bathing the room seem pale. She placed it on Bernard's chest, where it stuck to the cloth of his uniform without any pin being necessary. Then she drew near and, to the general's great astonishment, bestowed a light kiss on his lips. This done, she went off, gracious and dignified, followed by her escort.

The marshal was so surprised that it never even occurred to him to thank her.

"Well, you look just splendid with that," said his friend. "I don't doubt but you could easily get one hundred francs for that bauble on Earth—and then too, I must say they have such a delightful way of bestowing decorations in this country!"

"All right, there's no more time for jokes!" interrupted Bernard. "I must get back to the army as soon as possible, because something tells me the Kveyars are not going to wait long before showing themselves. When you've got the better of the epidemic, leave this planet and return to Dumyat. Whatever you do, don't let yourself be captured on the way. The Kveyars must remain ignorant of our existence for as long as possible. . . . Once you're back, report to me immediately. I don't like to be alone and—you're the only one I can confide in and in whom I have complete confidence, even though you don't always see things my way. I'm leaving you five ships as an escort. Goodbye."

The marshal-duke left the city under the globe and returned to the *Victory of Friedland*, which took off immediately, heading out into subspace and toward Dumyat.

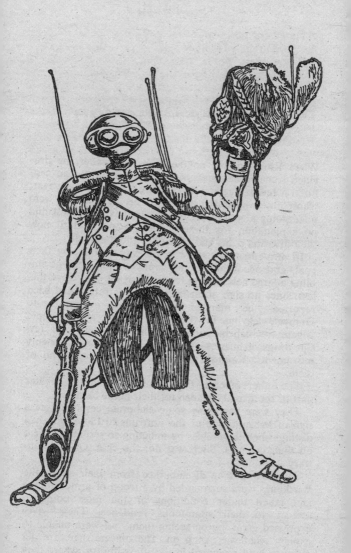

Chapter Eleven

When Kaninski was contacted by his leader, he provided some rather reassuring news. His craft had captured a few stragglers, and among them was a Kveyar, whose interrogation proved that his compatriots were undergoing a serious crisis because they could still find no explanation for these sudden reverses. Until now their invasion plans had gone off without a hitch.

In any case, they were in no way renouncing their goal, and according to the captive, they were assembling a large new fleet to try to finish the job. Nevertheless, since no sign of an enemy concentration had been reported, the marshal-duke decided to return to Dumyat, leaving in the Usk vicinity a few rapid frigates—which he considered the equivalent of a few squadrons of hussars—to keep him informed of enemy movements. Kaninski was to remain in command of them.

The other officers, the "brothers," and the greater part of the armada headed for their home base.

They were expecting some elaborate ceremony as a sign of the gratitude of the Fortruns to those who had distinguished themselves by inflicting so serious a defeat on their enemies. Such was not the case. On the contrary . . .

As soon as they disembarked from their ships, the Earthlings were surrounded by a troop of armed robots and taken under conditions of the most complete secrecy to their sumptuous residence. Their wives expressed great joy on seeing them, but were unable to explain what was going on. The officers therefore decided to hold a council in the study-library, where they were openly bitter as they celebrated their return with copious libations.

"It's unbelievable!" thundered Chastel, slamming his fist down on a fragile end table and causing it to splinter. "How ungrateful people are! We break our backs fighting to protect them and we're not even thanked for it."

"Ah! How very right you are!" agreed the chorus of Chastels. "We're not asking them to decorate us, but they could at least say thank you!"

"It's as though we didn't even exist. They seem to take us for robots!" exclaimed Bourief 6, whose stand was sustained by the exclamations of his brothers.

"Robots, that's the very word for it!" said the Queunots. "Once we're finished fighting, *hopla!* back in the box. . . ."

"I don't like this at all," emphasized Friancourt 3. "They're trying to make trouble for us. Our wives are so much alike that we have a devil of a time telling them apart! With the best intentions in the world, I almost grabbed for one of my sisters-in-law!"

"Bah!" put in Bernard 4. "It's just a question of working out the details. All we have to do is wear a number on our clothes, and there's no possible error!"

"What about at night?" asked Bernard 3 with a hearty laugh. "Do you want to mark their bottoms with indelible ink?"

"Why not?" Chastel 2 said approvingly. "I think it's a good idea!"

"All right, friends, let's get back to serious matters," interrupted the marshal-duke. "I admit that the attitude of the Fortruns surprises me a little, even though they've never exactly accustomed us to great demonstrations of gratitude. I have my own ideas about what's happening, and the Fortruns probably have some good reason for behaving this way."

"You're right!" approved Bernard 2. "As long as they still need us, there's nothing to fear."

"The only thing is," said Bernard 4, "I wouldn't be at all surprised if they play some dirty trick on us afterward."

Pierre Barbet

"Let's not get ahead of ourselves," interjected the marshal-duke. "I have already given a great deal of thought to that question. Until we have reason to think differently, we must not doubt that our hosts are well-disposed toward us. In any case, I have good reasons to be satisfied: first, because your conduct during the battle was worthy of the highest praise, and second, because our brothers seem to be integrating themselves into our little community remarkably well. Good Lord, you'd think we'd known each other for years! If we stick together, we've nothing to fear from whatever machinations the Fortruns may be planning."

The officers noisily manifested their approbation by immediately raising their glasses to their leader.

They had scarcely had time to empty them before the image of Ar'zog materialized in the center of the room.

"Glory and long life to your valiant space troopers!" proclaimed the Fortrun, in a pompous tone that was unusual for him. "My dear Bernard, you have just won a remarkable victory! Accept our thanks. I have good news for you. Our factories have produced a great number of spaceships to augment the forces under your command. I am convinced that with you at its head, this expanded fleet will liquidate the rabble that has dared to attack us. . . ."

"Thanks for your praise," growled the marshal-duke. "It strikes me as being a little late in coming, however. I thought you would have paid us the honor of receiving us at the astroport. Instead, you had us escorted here like so many criminals. Are you afraid we're becoming too popular?"

"I was expecting these reproaches, which have some justice behind them. But I want you to know that we've had good reasons for behaving this way. At this very moment, Dumyat is playing host to an important guest: Ernich, the Foreign Minister of the Olchiks. . . ."

"The Olchiks?" interrupted Bernard, knitting his brows. "I've never heard of those people. There was no mention of them in the hypno-pedagogical instruction!"

"That's true, my friend. They are a rough and hard-

130

working nomad people who live on the borders of the galaxy. Until now they have taken no part in the struggle between us and the Kveyars. They live in flying cities, going from planet to planet. Once the exploitation of a planet's resources is underway, their automatic factories pick up and move farther on. The planets they inhabit, with burned-out stars, generally no longer have any atmosphere. The conditions of life are difficult and comparable to those on the outer planets of your system: glacial climate, no sign of human life, but abundant mineral resources."

"Unbelievable!" exploded Bernard. "How can people be so sly? I'm given enormous responsibilities, launched into a difficult combat, and not even told the basic elements of the political context I'm working in!"

"You're right, and I understand your irritation. Nevertheless, put yourself in my place. Merely by calling you in, I was behaving in a revolutionary manner! I had to break the fundamental law which forbids all direct contact with underdeveloped peoples. Many of my compatriots thought it would be crazy to put so much power into your hands. You might very well have shown yourselves completely unscrupulous and attempted to overthrow my government. Who knows, you might even have simply tried to take us over.... I obtained the consent of our computers, but they did insist that we take certain precautions and in particular that you not be informed of all the factors in the problem. In this way we had certain guarantees."

"No doubt from time to time you make psychic soundings while we're asleep?"

Ar'zog was silent a moment and then continued:

"What difference does it make, after all? Yes, that's true. Besides, it's enabled us to confirm your loyalty and thus to assign larger forces to your command. Don't forget that our computers have many reservations about the empirical methods you use. According to them, we will one day or another run into a catastrophe. I had to plead your cause. The results you have obtained have been the best argument in your favor. You need have no fears insofar as that's concerned."

"What makes you think that I am willing to retain my command under such conditions?"

"It would be a serious error to abandon it. The success of the Kveyars would be as fatal for you as for us."

"Of course! In any case, I'm not one to do things by halves. You can count on me. Tell me about these Olchiks. What forces do they have at their disposal?"

"We have no very clear idea. Some think the fleet based in their flying cities is equal to that of the Kveyars, but generally speaking our computers have given us considerably lower figures—about half. However, we should remember that by constantly exploiting the resources of new planets, the Olchiks have constantly increased their power."

"Damn! And you left me in complete ignorance as to their existence! Can you imagine what would have happened if they had allied themselves with the Kveyars?"

"That's exactly the problem. Believe me, our computers have carefully examined the question. Until now, the Kveyars, thinking they would have no difficulty in conquering our planets, were not afraid of the Olchiks. But things have changed. Those rapacious Kveyars no longer hope to do away with our armies so quickly. They are not eager to fight on two fronts, and their ambassadors have offered to sign a nonaggression treaty with the Olchiks. They appear to have offered excellent terms, but Ernich wanted to consult with us before signing such an alliance. He is not unaware that if the Kveyars beat us, his own forces would then be confronted with an army of considerable size and equipment, which would make the situation dangerous for the Olchiks. On the other hand, he is in no way eager to see *us* win, as then the same problem would present itself. Our interest is therefore to see to it that for the time being the Olchiks remain neutral in this conflict. That is why it was extremely important that the ambassador know nothing about your existence. I hope you now understand the reasons for my behavior and my lack of courtesy."

"Hmm! All of that seems rather complicated,"

mumbled the marshal-duke. "And what do your computers have to say about it?"

"It was upon their advice that we kept your presence a secret. In that way our enemies' programming will be off, since it will not be able to take into account the new factor which you represent. . . ."

Ar'zog seemed pleased with the Machiavellian trick he was playing on both the Kveyars and the Olchiks. He positively quivered with pleasure.

"And what did you tell Ernich to explain the surprising success of your armies?"

"Simply that we've used more advanced computers than the Kveyars have, which is extremely plausible!"

"I assume that the Kveyars will be told about your conversations with Ernich?"

"No doubt about it! I think it reasonable to assume that they will then feel obliged to revise their equipment!"

"That's what I think, too. When will we be rid of this Ernich?"

"His spaceship has just taken off, and there is nothing more to fear. You are free to move about as before."

"I still say I would have liked to have had a part in these negotiations! What would have happened if the decisions you had taken had been contrary to my plans?"

The Fortrun immediately scowled.

"My friend, I think it best that we keep to the terms of our agreement. You have the direction of our armies and the right to name temporary governors—and even that, I emphasize, only on the planets you liberate. You have absolutely no say in any of the rest."

"Fine!" Bernard interrupted sharply. "But I warn you that if the Kveyars should manage to pull any tricks on me, you will have to bear the entire responsibility. It's impossible for me to judge a situation accurately if I don't know all the factors."

"Our computers have studied the question. They find you're managing very nicely as it is, at least for the moment. May I know what your plans are now that you have an even more powerful army, thanks to the recent reinforcements we've given you?"

"That's my business!" snapped the marshal. "According to our agreement, I am not obliged to inform you of my military plans."

"Quite right," replied Ar'zog, somewhat annoyed. "Well, then, my friend, I must leave you. Once more, my congratulations!"

The image of the Fortrun leader blurred and disappeared.

Bernard remained silent for a while and seemed to be thinking over what he had just learned. His companions respected his silence. Then, seeing that he remained sunk in his meditations, they discreetly slipped away for a rousing celebration of the Usk victory.

For a week the leader of the Fortrun armies remained closeted in his study. From time to time Tania and Friancourt would bring him meals or some coffee. Through the half-open door the officers could see maps of the galaxy and a desk piled high with papers covered by Bernard's nervous scrawl.

Finally, on the evening of the seventh day, the six original men were sent for. Only Faultrier, who was still at Usk, was absent.

The marshal-duke paced up and down the room, his hands clasped behind his back.

"Gentlemen," he declared, "we are going to set off on another campaign. Our enemies have still not had time to call in the troops massed on the borders near the Olchik territory. I know, however, that important movements are underway, since the Kveyars have the assurance of Olchik neutrality. I have decided to reorganize our forces. Let's begin with the most simple: you, Géraudont—you and Faultrier will take over complete responsibility for the army's expanded medical services. Faultrier will remain part of my headquarters staff, and I'm counting on you to see to it that our flying hospitals function smoothly."

"Thank you for your confidence, Marshal. I will do my best." Géraudont assured him. "After all, I don't have all that many humans to look after. One of the hospitals will be up on the front lines. The other will be in the rear areas."

"Good! And now to the combat units. I reserve the supreme command for myself. Each corps general, however, can take whatever action the necessities of the moment call for, provided that he keeps me informed of what he has done. Such initiatives must be of a minor nature and not interfere with the overall plan."

They all nodded their heads in approval and impatiently awaited what was to come next, but Bernard seemed in no hurry and was heightening the drama of the situation. He continued:

"As you have probably noticed, the ships placed at our disposal correspond reasonably well to the means utilized in armies on Earth. Fast and lightly armed corvettes are our chasseurs, the frigates are our hussars and dragoons. The cavalry is replaced by heavily armored vessels, not as fast as the others. As for the artillery, it has been replaced by missile launchers. Finally, the light vedettes with short-range laser-disintegrators can be compared to the infantry. It was by making use of such equivalences that I planned the battle of Usk.

"Here are the different army corps and their commanders. General Friancourt will direct our chasseurs, which will act as an advance guard for the rest of our forces; his brothers, will each command a company. Queunot 1 and his colonel-brothers will be responsible for the hussars. Kaninski will be in charge of the cavalry and will also command the dragoons. Bourief and Chastel, seconded by their brothers, will be responsible for the artillery. Finally, the infantry will be directed by both Bernard 2 and Géraudont 2, who will have under them Colonels Géraudont, Faultrier, and the other Bernards. You will note that our infantry is less important than in armies on Earth. I have worked out my plan of action. Instructions will be given to you on board your ships. I must emphasize that this time we will be faced with forces larger than those at Usk. That will be all. Thank you. You have fifteen minutes in which to get ready."

The officers immediately dispersed, and though they

were unhappy at having to once more leave their wives and this very comfortable château, they merely grumbled among themselves and in no way attempted to dispute their leader's orders.

Only Tania was so bold as to complain aloud.

"Why are we pursued by this fatal scourge? On Earth our poor isbas were pillaged, the cattle stolen, the fields laid waste, and my family scattered. Here, we might have hoped to find peace. We have a magnificent home, we could be happy.... And now our husbands have to leave us once more and go off to battle. For days on end we will have to wait for news of them, trembling for their lives. It must be that there is a curse on humans...."

"Don't worry, my love," Bernard said reassuringly. "Our ships are never on the front line, and we are in considerably less danger than we were on Earth. Besides, Faultrier and Géraudont have remarkable equipment with which to care for us if it should be necessary. Anyhow, given the Fortrun duplicators, you have nothing to fear. If I disappear, they will replace me with a synthetic twin and you will never know the difference!"

"That's what you think! May God grant that it never be put to the test. No matter what happens, these cursed creatures will never come near me. They are diabolic creations, phantoms that trick our senses. Things like that are against the law of God. You, you alone, are my husband. I love you, and nobody will ever take your place!"

Bernard trailed a lingering finger along the gentle curve of her soft cheek, pausing for a moment over a dimple, as though to better remember this beloved face, and then he said:

"Perhaps you're right.... In any case, I promise to be careful. Courage! Everything will work itself out and we will be able to enjoy this magnificent dwelling in peace. But before we can, the Kveyars must be destroyed. Have faith in me: I am going to see to it. Soon these separations will be only a bad memory...."

Eager to get the farewell over with, the marshal

bestowed a kiss on Tania's forehead and went off without looking back. His wife made no effort to retain him, but large tears flowed down her cheeks. She was far from feeling the same optimism and feared that all these battles would certainly end badly.

The majestic takeoff of the Fortrun armed forces did not go unnoticed. For hours on end the ships left the planet as the air bellowed against their hulls. Ar'zog came to say good-bye to the marshal-duke, and the Fortrun's compatriots, their habitual ennui disturbed, seemed to realize that this time it was their very destiny that would be at stake in the days to come. They uneasily raised their heads to contemplate this splendid spectacle, and hurriedly treated themselves to a dose of some euphoria-inspiring preparation in order to lift their morale.

A few vessels were reported by the detectors of the lead ships to be lingering off Dumyat. It was Ambassador Ernich and his escort, who were making an estimate of the size of the squadrons being sent off against the Kveyars.

This was extremely disagreeable, and the marshal would not tolerate it. He therefore sent several ships in the direction of these intruders and ordered Queunot to set up a smoke screen between the Olchiks and his fleet. The intruders took the hint and headed out into space without wasting any time.

Bernard found that he really didn't like those people and that he was very suspicious of them. However, he was careful not to pursue them, since their intervention in the coming campaign would obviously be catastrophic.

For a few hours the different army corps circled around Dumyat getting into battle formation. The marshal-duke took advantage of this interval to put the final touches to his plans; however, from time to time he glanced up at the viewing screens, unable to keep from admiring the spectacle of this multitude of spaceships of all sizes and shapes silhouetted against the velvety sky.

When all his generals had signaled they were ready,

137

the commander in chief of the Fortrun armed forces gave the order to move into twelve-dimensional subspace and head for their destination: the planet Agram, which was situated on the former frontier of the empire.

Now it was important to make every effort to keep the army's destination secret. Because of this, orders were given to the lead ships to stop all vessels they encountered on their way to the Kveyar territories, place Fortrun crews aboard, and send the ships to Dumyat.

Ar'zog would probably not care for this measure, taken without his consent, and would liberate the vessels with lame excuses. But by the time this happened, they would have lost all trace of the fleet, and that was what counted. In any case, if the coming battle turned to his advantage, Bernard planned to establish a general blockade of the planets occupied by the Kveyars so that he could cut off their supplies of raw materials and thus lower their ship production. But that was another matter—part of the marshal-duke's vast projects.

The only incident that occurred during the journey was the arrival of a vessel from Usk. It received authorization to come alongside the *Victory of Friedland.* On board were Faultrier and several Uskians, among whom Bernard was surprised to see the Princess Hina.

"Madame," he declared in a reproachful tone, "you do me great honor in coming here. However, I cannot permit you to take such a risk. Everybody would blame me, and justly so, if I were to expose you to danger in this way. I ask that you return to the rear areas so that your life will not be endangered."

"I would be ashamed to behave in so cowardly a fashion! Am I to remain in safety while you fight to preserve my country from slavery? My people are peace-loving and until now have been concerned only with the arts, but we know that we must fight to defend our liberty when need arises. I can learn much faster at your side. Besides, I would rather die than fall under the Kveyar yoke once more!"

"As you wish. However, I must inform you that I

will have very little time for you. Faultrier will explain how I am carrying out the operation as we go along. . . . And now tell me, old friend, were you able to complete your mission successfully?"

"Unfortunately, we had a great many more deaths to grieve over before the arrival of the ship loaded with medical supplies," sighed the chief surgeon. "However, the fungicide worked marvels. The epidemic is definitely wiped out, but one in every three Uskians died. . . ."

"They will be avenged, I promise you!" cried Princess Hina. "I have good news for you, Marshal. The Uskians have decided to make a contribution to the struggle for liberation that is about to take place. It's a little apparatus developed from the polyfrequency organs we use to broadcast our concerts. With it, you can jam the hyper-radio communications of enemy spaceships. It also makes it possible to jumble the electronic brains of robots and even of computers. However, for that you need a reasonably powerful unit. As you can see, the inconvenience of my presence aboard will be compensated for in some measure. . . ."

"Princess Hina, you have just given me a magnificent gift! This is going to handicap our enemies considerably. Can you equip several of my ships with this marvelous scrambler?"

"I've brought about twenty of them with me, and my technicians will teach you to make others."

"That will be more than I need! Be sure that the secret of their very existence is carefully guarded. Are you certain that neither the Kveyars nor the Fortruns have similar devices?"

"I can assure you they don't."

"Then this is the most magnificent gift I have received since I arrived here. Faultrier, have one of these distributed to each of my generals. And make sure that one such device is installed on board this ship immediately! We're going to give these damn Kveyars quite a nasty surprise! Now I'm sure that we will cut them to pieces!"

"Hina, you have proved to me that gratitude is not an empty word. Your alliance will make it possible for me to carry out plans which were close to my heart, but which I thought were very likely impossible. . . ."

"You can count on me, Marshal. No matter what happens, I will never forget that thanks to your help my people escaped a terrible death!"

Chapter Twelve

All the corps commanders received a Uskian scrambler, and soon the lead ships made contact with the Kveyar forces.

The reports that flooded the marshal-duke's headquarters showed that the struggle would be a heated one. The enemy easily outnumbered them. Positioned in an arc formation, the Kveyars were awaiting the attackers. Bernard quickly took in the fact that they had massed considerable strength on the two wings in hopes of catching the Fortruns in a pincer movement and closing the trap. The outcome of this battle was of supreme importance to each of the opposing sides.

The time had come to recall certain essential principles of the Emperor Napoleon. Large armies, he used to say, cannot advance in a single column without the risk of having their heads bashed in by the enemy; several columns are necessary. Bernard therefore separated his forces into three principle groups, reserving the command of the one in the center for himself. He confided the left wing to Kaninski, the right to Queunot. The scouts were placed in the center and put under Friancourt's command.

Bourief and Chastel—with the artillery, the missile launchers—were positioned slightly to the rear on either side of the center. By doing this, Bernard was following another of the Emperor's precepts: though there should be only one commanding general per army, in a large battle there should be at least five army corps; the greater part of the artillery should be with the infantry divisions and the heavy cavalry must be out front and on the wings so that it could support the light cavalry.

The marshal-duke had given a great deal of thought

to these principles and felt that he was now applying them perfectly to the conditions of space combat.

The Kveyars assuredly knew nothing about the fine points of the art of war and merely carried out the tactics dictated by their computers; keeping their preceding defeats in mind, they attacked on the two wings.

From the very beginning of the battle, General Friancourt was ordered to fall back and take up positions before the artillery units of Bourief and Chastel; he was to be in the center and to limit himself to defensive action.

On the left, General Kaninski, supported by the infantry of Géraudont 2, courageously absorbed the shock and, better yet, was able to drive the enemy back and oblige it to bring reinforcements from the center to continue the attack. The same was true of the right wing, where Queunot and the infantry under Bernard 2 accomplished miracles.

Once again the Kveyars had to call on troops from the center for reinforcements.

From his position in the heart of the battle, Bernard followed the operations on a vast spherical radar screen on which he could easily see the opposing movements of the blue spots of light, his own men, as well as those of the Kveyars, who were represented by red spots of light. He decided that the moment had come to go onto the offensive, and he launched Friancourt's regiments at the Kveyar center.

As far as the eye could see, space was ablaze with the firing of the combatants—the purple streaks of the infantry disintegrators, the bluish flashes of the "cuirassiers'" weapons, and the dazzling explosions of the missiles, particularly dense on the two flanks. The units sped forward, firing broadside after broadside.

The immediate effect of Friancourt's attack was to bring Kveyar troops toward the center as fast as they could move in order to defend this weakened point. Suddenly, Queunot and Kaninski, the pressure off them, could in turn go over to the offensive on the wings; but they could make little progress under the fire of the enemy's missile-artillery.

Nor could the "dragoons" long profit from their initial advantage, and they fell back on their original positions in front of the batteries of Bourief and Chastel.

The Kveyars exulted. For the first time in a long while the enemy was unable to break through their lines and advance. The Kveyars therefore moved all the available troops over to the center in a determined effort to finish things as quickly as possible.

A sly smile spread over the marshal-duke's craggy face when he saw the Kveyar offensive taking shape on his viewing screen. He immediately ordered General Friancourt to take up positions behind the Bourief and Chastel batteries, and in this way avoid the brutal shock of the assault. Then a code message was sent to all the corps commanders to put their Uskian scramblers into operation. Once this was done the Kveyars would be unable to learn what was happening and therefore unable to direct their armies.

The first enemy waves—formed of cavalry, dragoons, and hussars, according to the way Bernard considered them, but in reality frigates and corvettes—were right under the fire of the missile-launcher artillery. They were immediately annihilated. The cuirassiers who followed plunged in turn into this inferno, and very few of them survived.

The batteries of Bourief and Chastel fired away happily, launching an unremitting hail of projectiles. The Kveyar infantry, which had swarmed forth after its cavalry, thinking that the cavalry had surely reached and put the missile launchers out of action, was itself caught in a tornado of flames. Atomic explosions annihilated the serried ranks of the light armored units before they could even come within firing range of the Fortrun lines.

It was a veritable massacre, but the worst of it was that the Kveyars, though they knew the battle was intense, were unable to find out just what was happening, and they launched all their reserves in wave after wave. This made it possible for General Friancourt to plunge into the weakened center and sweep the few survivors before him.

The enemy center no longer existed, but the Kveyar commanders whose communications had been totally disrupted, did not know this.

With the great ease, Kaninski and Queunot were able to return to the offensive on the wings. Initially the Kveyars fell back in good order, but then they broke and found themselves between two lines of fire, as Friancourt had split his forces in two and was attacking their rear.

Once this happened, the battle was lost. The survivors of the Kveyar armada panicked and had only one desire—to break out and escape.

The battle ended in a number of chaotic engagements in which Marshal Bernard's rapid units had trouble keeping on the heels of the fleeing enemy.

According to initial estimates, almost half the Kveyar armies were destroyed or captured. The "dragoons" and the "hussars" kept overtaking and capturing the slower of the enemy combatants, who, for the most part, had no idea of what was happening.

At this point, Bernard received a message from Ar'zog. Its import was quite clear: given the numerical inferiority of the marshal's forces, the computers forbade him to enter into a battle whose outcome was uncertain, and they instructed him to retreat in good order!

Bernard exploded: "Well, that's good to know," he declared to Hina. "I've disobeyed these idiotic orders and I'm not any the worse for it. It's true that luck was on my side: your scramblers were of inestimable help, and good old Ar'zog computers knew nothing about them. . . . It reminds me of what my venerated leader, the Emperor Napoleon, used to say: there are two kinds of campaign plans, good one and bad ones. Sometimes the good ones fail due to accidents, sometimes the bad ones succeed thanks to a whim of fortune . . . but you have to know how to profit from anything that happens. Fortune is a woman; if you miss out today, don't expect to get another chance tomorrow."

"That Earthling was a sage," noted the princess, "and his precepts seem quite judicious to me. I would like to know if he also foresaw what would happen to a victorious leader whose power was feared!"

"Of course," replied the marshal immediately. "In the Year VIII—1799, according to the way dates are now noted—on the eighteen Brumaire, when Napoleon appeared before the Council of the Five Hundred he was greeted with shouts of 'Death to the tyrant! down with the dictator!' Some of those present tried to plunge their daggers into him. His grenadiers intervened and his brother Lucien exclaimed: 'Wretches! You want me to outlaw my brother, savior of the country, the man whose name makes kings tremble! I relinquish the badges of popular magistrateship.' Napoleon was then named First Consul and immediately set about seizing absolute power. Yes, Princess, I am fully aware of the risks I run now that the Kveyars are no longer a serious threat. Ar'zog and his clique are going to try to put me and my generals out of the way. Their computers find that I'm dangerous, and they are perfectly correct. The only thing is that I'm afraid they were a little late in discovering this. I am going to reenter Dumyat at the head of my army and present myself before them. My faithful officers will accompany me with your scramblers, and I guarantee you that I will not let the opportunity to seize power slip by. Can I count on you?"

Hina nodded her head in affirmation.

"I think I have already assured you that no matter what, I can refuse nothing to the man who saved my people," she said simply.

"That's a promise then. Head for Dumyat!"

And while the ships maneuvered to get into columns, Bernard proceeded to some well-deserved promotions and awards. Queunot was made Duke of Agram and given sovereignty over all the planets of that stellar system. Friancourt, the courageous redhead, received the Legion of Honor, and Kaninski was presented the Seven-Pointed Star, from the hand of the princess herself.

This done, the marshal-duke sent a message to Ar'zog telling him that he had entered into combat and decimated his adversaries. The Dumyat station acknowledged receipt of the message but did not comment on it.

During the trip back, Hina apprised Bernard of many things. The real leaders of the Fortruns were the computers, he learned, and the notables were simply their spokesmen. The exercise of power was too boring to these sybarites for them to attach any real importance to it. They demanded only one thing: to enjoy in peace the life, pleasures, and intoxication assured them by subtle drugs. The cyborgs were only puppets, without energy and ambition.

In addition, Hina emphasized that the Olchiks, far from being peace-loving, had ambitions comparable to those of the Kveyars. They had just made an alliance with the Itains—a people living in a stellar kingdom surrounded on all sides by nearly impenetrable nebulas—and they were now only waiting for the outcome of the current conflict to rush in for the kill.

Once forewarned, Bernard immediately issued a general order to all the patrols of the two army corps speeding toward the Kveyar capital under Kaninski's command: every cargo ship they encountered was to be boarded and seized. A total blockade was needed to isolate the Itains and the Olchiks. They were to receive no more supplies of raw material and no more news about what was happening to the Kveyars. Bernard, of course, had no illusions about the effectiveness of this blockade: these two nations had ample riches to insure that the first measure would have very little effect on them; however, the second—the news blackout—would be considerably more troublesome, as it would leave them in total ignorance of how the situation was developing.

Escorted by twenty ships, the *Victory of Friedland* landed at the Dumyat astroport without encountering any opposition. Bernard disembarked along with his generals and one hundred armed robots.

He had scarcely gone a hundred meters before a strong detachment of hovercars surrounded him and his escort. Its leader, a robot, declared he had orders to bring the marshal and his generals before the notables.

Bernard smilingly agreed and then started up his scramblers.

The soliders under Ar'zog's orders were immediately replaced by an equal number of his own: the others, disconnected by the field disrupter, were transported into the ships.

Next the cortege set off for the vast hall where the assembly which represented the outward power of the Fortruns met. Encircled by robots as though they were prisoners, the Earthmen made their entrance into the room where Ar'zog sat surrounded by his peers, all draped in long purple togas and coiffed with transmitters that looked like caps.

The accused were placed in an empty dock and the robot escort formed a circle around them.

Ar'zog stood up and turned his eyestalks on the Earthlings. Bernard appeared relaxed, glancing casually around the hall and admiring the magnificent bas-reliefs that decorated the walls. A solemn and moving anthem, composed of extremely beautiful musical motifs, was heard, and then the leader of the Fortruns began to speak.

"Marshal Bernard," he declared in a rancorous tone, "I suppose you know why you have been convoked before our sovereign assembly?"

"I am honored, but I have no idea of why I am here," the Earthling assured him.

Ar'zog looked at him a moment and then manipulated the buttons of an apparatus attached to his belt before grumbling:

"That's true! Astonishing as it may be, this probe registers your surprise, and is unimaginable that a primitive being like yourself could oppose a mental barrier to its investigations. Well, then, I will tell you why you are here. The Council has summoned you because you are accused of having on several occasions broken our agreements. First, by ordering the cargo ships of all nationalities seized without having previously asked our authorization. This serious omission would be enough to condemn you, but there is even more—an intolerable insubordination on your part. You received a message forbidding you to enter into combat with numerically superior forces and yet you went ahead!"

"Obviously," protested Bernard, "since the order didn't reach me until after the battle. . . ."

We have incontrovertible proof that it was sent before your forces were committed. In any case, you had only to withdraw and refrain from combat."

"Well, well. Imagine that," said the marshal with a loud laugh.

"You are pleased to scoff, my friend! Well, you will change your tune when you realize that the crimes of lese majesty are punishable by death for you and all your accomplices, including every one of your identical twins."

"In other words, all the Earthlings. . . ."

"That is correct! What have you to say in your defense?"

"Oh, not a great deal. It certainly wouldn't be of much use, since it is obvious that your computers have found that we were becoming dangerous and that it was time to get rid of us. It's not very loyal of you, for after all we never asked to come here—it was you who came to search for us on Earth. In addition, I have accomplished what you wanted: the Kveyars have been beaten and will no doubt soon sue for peace. By this time, the army corps I have sent in pursuit of them must be near their capital."

"Let us stick to the accusations! Do you admit your guilt?"

"Yes, insofar as the capture of cargo ships is concerned. I might add that I have extended that order to cover the Itains. No, as to the second charge. I did not know of your prohibition against engaging combat until after the battle."

"Your denial is worthless. Our signal centers have assured us of the contrary!"

"If you're so sure, why ask me?"

"Impertinent! Since you insist on mocking this assembly, we will immediately proceed to a vote on the following question: Is Marshal-Duke Bernard disloyal and a criminal? If yes, then he and his Earthling accomplices are to suffer the death penalty, the sentence to be carried out immediately."

The Fortruns then pressed one of the two buttons before them, and two hundred affirmative votes were immediately registered on a luminous panel.

"Robots, take the condemned men away!" grated Ar'zog.

At this point, Bernard and his companions again put their scramblers into operation and trained them on the venerable assembly. All the cyborgs, with one motion, raised their clawlike hands to their heads as though racked by intolerable pain, and then they tumbled over like so many ninepins struck by a bowling ball. The delicate mechanisms charged with mediating between their brains—resting in a downy receptacle—and their metal bodies were agitated by powerful short circuits.

"Robots, take them away!" Bernard laughed. "Put them in a cargo ship and dispatch it into orbit five hundred kilometers up. Chastel, take command of their escort."

"At your orders," chortled the big Alsatian, happy to be assigned this mission.

This memorable Council meeting ended on this note.

The marshal-duke did not forget the tender Hina's warnings. The euphoria of the moment did not make him lose sight of the fact that this band of puppets represented only the illusion of power. He still had to deal with the computers.

The oniro-educator training had not, of course, taught the Earthlings where these mysterious machines were located. This was no insurmountable obstacle, however, and the well-stocked library of the Council of Notables proved to contain numerous psycho-reels that furnished all the necessary information.

Bernard spent an enjoyable interval there, but what he learned only emphasized the difficulties that awaited him. The giant electronic brains were entrenched below the city, more than a hundred meters under the ground! Only a few robots responsible for their maintenance could come near them. To assure themselves total autonomy, they had even established a private power-house enclosed in an impregnable shelter.

For the first time since the beginning of his mad enterprise, Bernard felt the shadow of defeat over him. But it would really to be too idiotic to fail now that victory was so close at hand. . . .

The marshal's indomitable energy and optimism soon got the upper hand again. There was one way to make it impossible for his unknown enemies to do him any harm. Followed by his escort, the Marshal-Duke of Ariman started for the underground passages leading to the lair of the electronic monsters.

An anti-g shaft took him to the armored door guarded by robots. The scramblers soon took care of them.

Then he was faced with a new problem. How was he to open this indestructible gate forged from the most resistant alloys? Extraordinary cohesion was accomplished by a steel with a molecular structure that eliminated all space between the atoms. . . .

Very quickly, the solution came to him: a psycho-prober applied to one of the robot guards provided the combination of the Hertzian lock, and the last obstacle gave way before the adventurer from Earth.

After this it was relatively easy to reach the giant computers. Warned of the arrival of the intruders, the computers sent additional robot squads against them, but they met the same fate the others had. The scramblers turned them into a harmless heap of junk. Bernard then entered one of the cubicles reserved to the Fortrun notables, cubicles in which they used to receive the orders of their infallible machines. From this position, he could see the computers and was able to establish contact with the true masters of Dumyat. He put on a communications helmet and declared:

"Your reign is over! Until now, abject creatures accepted the domination of machines which should never have gone beyond the status of entities capable of giving advice and counsel. I, Bernard, a man of flesh and blood who comes from Earth, am about to put an end to your usurped power. Henceforth, I shall be the only master of the destiny of the Fortruns."

A response that betrayed no sign of bitterness—it was, in fact, almost disinterested in tone—reached him immediately.

"We were wrong to underestimate you. Obviously, Earthlings possess to the highest degree the ability to adapt to even the most unusual circumstances. Your success in the war against the Kveyars proves it, and the fact that you were able to get to us demonstrates it in an even more dazzling manner. We would very much like to know your methods, but it seems certain that you will keep them secret. An unforeseen factor interfered with our plans, and that is our excuse—though we have no real need to justify ourselves. An impenetrable psychic barrier makes it impossible to probe your thoughts, otherwise you would quickly have been made unable to harm us. Alas, the examination of your cerebral structure did not allow us to discover this in sufficient time. What are you going to do to us?"

"I am not about to destroy such wonderfully perfected machines," the marshal-duke assured them. "For the moment, I am going to make use of apparatus whose existence you know nothing of: scramblers will make it impossible for you to function normally. Later, teams of robot technicians will modify your control centers so that they have no free will and you once more become what you should always have been: servants of creatures of flesh and blood."

"We realize there is no appeal from this decision. However, you ought to know that you have won only one round of this game of cosmic chess. Others will avenge us! Your limited brains will never be able to carry out your vast projects. A human being will never dominate the galaxy. Accursed be . . ."

Bernard had heard enough, and he pressed the button of the powerful scrambler he had brought with him.

"Electronic brothers of the far stars . . . beware of the Earthli . . . Their leader Bernard . . . psychic characteris . . . 789 896 A 2 . . . the square of the hypotenuse is equal . . . rights . . . the cologarithm is equal to . . . all psi ... neutron presence ... the relation . . equipotential ... ooon ..."

The psychic message sounded far off, became incoherent, and progressively faded.

A gleam of triumph shone from the Earthling's eyes. He had just heard the death rattle of his last adversaries. By his determination, his perseverance, an intelligence as limited as his own had just triumphed over the most subtly perfected achievements of the galaxy. Now nothing separated him from the supreme title: Emperor of the Fortrun Planets.

Epilogue

With the help of the Uskian technicians and of the Princess Hina, his faithful ally, the Marshal-Duke of Ariman spent the following days shoring up his still fragile power.

The robots were conditioned to obey only his orders, and the circuits of the computers themselves were modified so as to deprive the electronic brains of all personal initiative.

Then Kaninski sent a triumphant message: the Kveyars had just signed a peace treaty! His forces had already occupied their capital. The government was in flight and asked that it be allowed to negotiate immediately with an authorized representative of the Fortruns.

Bernard signaled his willingness, and a ship carrying the Kveyar ambassadors arrived at Dumyat. The surprise of those aboard was total: they had understood that human beings from somewhere had been employed as mercenaries and were directing the army that had beaten them, but they had never imagined these humans had taken power....

The peace treaty was quickly ratified. In it the marshal-duke showed himself magnanimous and only a few of the key planets situated on the frontiers were annexed. The Kveyars recognized the rule of the Earthling over the Fortrun empire. They also accepted the clauses concerning a total blockade of Olchik and Itain possessions. In case of war with these peoples, the Kveyars were to take a stance of friendly neutrality and furnish subsidies to the Fortrun armies. Finally, they agreed to send a delegation to the celebration at which the marshal-duke would be anointed emperor.

The preparations for this event began immediately. Uskian artists sent by Princess Hina, who had returned to her planet, arrived to decorate and to provide music for the imperial residence. Sumptuous robes were sewn. Many Fortruns, always hungry for pleasure, collaborated in working out the ceremony. They wholeheartedly accepted the rise of their new leader. Bernard was careful to allow them free use of the drugs and many other commodities they could not do without, and that was all these indolent people demanded.

Finally, the great day arrived.

To legitimize this solemn rite, Bernard had pardoned Ar'zog and the notables on the condition that they take an oath of allegiance and fidelity to him. The enormous oniro-suggester auditorium had been chosen for the ceremony. All the preparations had been carefully worked out by moving little figurines about on a table.

Colorfully dressed delegations came from all parts of the empire to honor their new master. Ambassadors and diplomats from every point on the galactic compass were there, including Ernich himself. The Uskians, of course, were the most numerous and the most enthusiastic.

The wives of the generals, dukes, and colonels, all dressed in silver-embroidered robes, surrounded the future empress—the poor Russian peasant who was about to be apotheosized. They helped her put on her lavish finery. Her dress came from the most fashionable Uskian couturier. Spidery laces, gold embroidery, dazzling gems, inestimably heightened her charms. Tania put on slippers garnished with blue pearls and she wore gloves of an iridescent cloth. On her head was placed a diadem of multifaceted gems that shone like so many miniature suns. Jewels sparkled from her ears, her throat, her fingers, emphasizing the whiteness of her skin. Nobody on Earth would have been able to give a name to these gems, but any jeweler would have paid a fortune for the least of them.

Bernard came to rejoin his wife in the Malmaison salon. His clothes were patterned after those he had seen worn by Napoleon: swan-white satin culottes embroidered with gold, a coat of purple velvet, a red cape decorated with laurel leaves and golden bees. From his side hung a sword whose hilt was carved from a block of jasper and into whose pommel was set an enormous diamond.

His faithful officers, as dazzlingly attired as their wives, were waiting. As usual, Kaninski's costume was the most extravagant.

The cortege started for the gilt-covered hovercars that were awaiting them. The imperial "carriage" could easily be distinguished from the others: on its roof were four giant eagles with laurel branches clutched in their claws. A golden crown glowed in the center. As an added refinement, and so as not to disappoint the faithful beasts, five very useless horses were attached to it. They were led, of course, by the worthy Volant, who pranced about proudly, his head covered with plumes.

Salvos of missiles began to thunder as the vehicles started up. The carriage was preceded by the entire general staff, with Kaninski at their head; they were immediately followed by eight squadrons of robots lustily sounding their trumpets and cymbals. Behind came the richly decorated hovercars of the ladies.

After a triumphant parade under the somewhat mocking eyes of the Fortruns, who did not much care for the barbarous accents of the fanfares, the cortege halted before the vast edifice where the ceremony was to be held.

An interminable procession penetrated the immense hall as the polyphonic organs of the Uskians played a coronation march especially composed for the occasion; the Fortruns gathered there seemed to be delighted with it.

Bernard 2 and Bernard 3 carried the train of their brother's robe. Behind came the generals, who were followed by their respective brothers.

The imperial couple sat down on the two covered thrones on the dais and the ceremony began.

Before them stood Ar'zog with the imperial ornaments—the sword, globe, scepter, and two crowns resting on embroidered cushions. He was sitting on a throne slightly lower than those of the Earthlings.

He solemnly pronounced the formula of allegiance and the pledges, then he picked up the imperial crown and attempted to place it on Bernard's head; but the Earthling, imitating Napoleon, quickly seized it and placed it on his head with his own hands.

The organs thundered forth.

Friancourt held out the sword, Queunot the collar of the Legion of Honor, Bourief the globe, and Chastel the scepter.

Kaninski presented Tania's crown and Bernard placed it on the head of his imperial spouse.

Finally, Faultrier covered the shoulders of the two new majesties with a mantle of purple velvet and cried in a loud voice: *"Vivat Imperator in aeternum!"*

The wives of the dignitaries brushed aside hypocritical tears even as in their secret hearts they envied the glory of their friend.

The chorus of generals replied to Faultrier with: "Long live the Emperor! Long live the Empress!"

But their shouts were immediately drowned out by the salvo of a hundred missiles whose mission it was to inform the good Fortruns that they now had an emperor. . . .

The ceremony over, the cortege returned to the carriages and, after long detours through the arteries of Dumyat, the celebrants disembarked at Malmaison.

That evening there were festivities attended by both the Earthlings and the Fortruns. In a sky illuminated by satellites, artificial dawn spread shimmering ribbons of light.

A gargantuan supper was served in the salons of the imperial residence, and a ball terminated the evening. The Russian women and their husbands were able to give full vent to their warm temperaments.

Late that night, the imperial couple ascended to their apartments as the guests shouted hurrahs.

Within a week the emperor had reactivated his legions and presented them with the Stellar Eagles.

Behind him, Faultrier pensively observed the ceremony and wondered where his friend's thirst for conquest would end.

The surgeon would have given several years of his life to know. ...

Presenting MICHAEL MOORCOCK
in DAW editions

Presenting C. J. CHERRYH

☐ **DOWNBELOW STATION.** A blockbuster of a novel! Interstellar warfare as humanity's colonies rise in cosmic rebellion. (#UE1594—$2.75)

☐ **SERPENT'S REACH.** Two races lived in harmony in a quarantined constellation—until one person broke the truce! (#UE1682—$2.50)

☐ **FIRES OF AZEROTH.** Armageddon at the last gate of three worlds. (#UJ1466—$1.95)

☐ **HUNTER OF WORLDS.** Triple fetters of the mind served to keep their human prey in bondage to this city-sized starship. (#UE1559—$2.25)

☐ **BROTHERS OF EARTH:** This in-depth novel of an alien world and a human who had to adjust or die was a Science Fiction Book Club Selection. (#UJ1470—$1.95)

☐ **THE FADED SUN: KESRITH.** Universal praise for this novel of the last members of humanity's warrior-enemies . . . and the Earthman who was fated to save them. (#UE1692—$2.50)

☐ **THE FADED SUN: SHON'JIR.** Across the untracked stars to the forgotten world of the Mri go the last of that warrior race and the man who had betrayed humanity.
(#UE1753—$2.50)

☐ **THE FADED SUN: KUTATH.** The final and dramatic conclusion of this bestselling trilogy—with three worlds in militant confrontation. (#UE1743—$2.50)

☐ **HESTIA.** A single engineer faces the terrors and problems of an endangered colony planet. (#UE1680—$2.25)

Presenting JOHN NORMAN in DAW editions ...